Honey

Trixie Belden

Your
TRIXIE BELDEN
Library

Trixie Belden

and the
MYSTERIOUS
VISITOR

by Julie Campbell

Illustrated by Marvin Besunder

Cover by Paul Frame

WHITMAN PUBLISHING COMPANY • Racine, Wisconsin

CONTENTS

**The
Mysterious
Visitor**

1

An Unhappy Friend

TRIXIE AND HONEY linked arms as they left their home-room. "Oh, woe," Trixie moaned. "Homework on a Friday. It's not fair. It'll ruin the whole weekend." She was a sturdy girl of thirteen with short sandy curls and round blue eyes. "Every October since I learned to write," she complained, "the English teacher has given us the same old assignment." Trixie frowned, looked down her nose, and said in a high-pitched voice: " 'Now, children, I want you to tell me in not less than two hundred words what you did this summer.' Phooey! If I hand in a hundred words, I'll be doing well. And they're all sure to be spelled wrong and not punctuated properly."

Honey Wheeler, who was Trixie's best friend,

laughed. She had earned her nickname because of her golden-brown hair, and she had wide hazel eyes. Although they were the same age, Honey was taller and slimmer than Trixie. "You couldn't possibly," she said, "tell about everything we did this summer, Trixie, in a *million* words. I thought we'd divide up our exciting experiences. Since he's my adopted brother now, I'll tell how we found Jim up at the old mansion and lost him, and then found him again when we solved the red trailer mystery. You could tell about the diamond we found in the gatehouse, and the thieves who stole it from us, and how you helped the police capture them."

Trixie sniffed. "Telling about something is one thing; writing about it is another. I never could write about things and make them sound interesting—not even when I was very interested in them myself. My fingers ache at the very thought of holding a pencil long enough to explain all about the gatehouse and the diamond and the thieves and everything. And how the gatehouse is our secret clubhouse now. Of course, I'd never tell that part of the story, anyway."

"I should hope not." Although it was the last week of October, it was a very warm day. Honey pushed her bangs back from her forehead with her free hand. "You shouldn't even talk about our club in the corridor when so many kids are milling around." She lowered her voice to a whisper. "Suppose someone guessed that the initials B.W.G. stand for Bob-Whites of the Glen? Oh, Trixie, wasn't it fun the first day of school when we wore our special red jackets and just baffled everyone?"

Trixie nodded. "I don't know how you ever made those jackets so quickly, Honey. And as for cross-stitching B.W.G. on the backs in white, well *that* baffled *me*. As far as I'm concerned, all sewing is cross-stitching because every time I look a needle in the eye I feel cross."

Honey hugged Trixie's arm. "As long as we're neighbors, you don't even have to think about sewing. I'll always do your mending for you, Trix. I just love to sew, and mending is no trouble at all."

The girls lived on Glen Road which was about two miles from the junior-senior high school in the village of Sleepyside-on-the-Hudson. They and Jim Frayne and Trixie's older brothers, Brian and Mart, traveled to and from school by bus. The Manor House, which was the name of the Wheelers' huge estate, included acres of rolling lawn and woodlands, a big lake, and a stable of handsome horses. It formed the western boundary of the Beldens' Crabapple Farm, which nestled down in a hollow. Honey's home was luxurious and very beautiful, but Trixie preferred the pretty little white frame house where she lived with her three brothers and their parents.

"I hope we'll always be neighbors," she said to Honey. "I would have died of loneliness last summer if your father hadn't bought the Manor House. There was just no one around to talk to. Brian and Mart were away at camp and there was nobody left but Bobby. And you can't do things with him. Just keep him out of trouble—if possible—and wash his face and comb his hair and bandage his scraped knees. That's not a very exciting way to spend a whole summer, let me tell you."

"I know someone who's dying of loneliness right now," Honey said thoughtfully. "And I feel awfully sorry for her."

"Who?" Trixie asked curiously. With the exception of Honey, she had gone to grade school with all of the boys and girls who had entered junior high that September. She couldn't think of one of them who had any reason for being lonely. Most of them lived in the pretty residential section of the town which sprawled along the east bank of the Hudson River. Because they lived so near one another, they had grand times after school and during the holidays, whereas, almost all of the bus children were separated from their friends by miles or at least acres. "Who?" Trixie asked again.

14

"Diana Lynch," Honey said, whispering.

"Di—lonely?" Trixie was so surprised that she almost shouted.

"Sh-h," Honey cautioned. "She might be right behind us."

"Why, she's got everything," Trixie continued in a slightly lower voice. "Next to you, Honey, she's the prettiest girl in our class. She doesn't get very good marks, but neither do I. She's got two sets of twins for brothers and sisters, and her father made a million dollars a couple of years ago. They have a huge place that's as gorgeous as yours, high up on a hill that's even higher than your hill, with a marvelous view of the river. I've only been out there once, but—"

"That's the point," Honey interrupted. "Why haven't you been out there more than once? Why doesn't she ever sit near you on the bus? I thought you and Di had known each other since kindergarten."

"We have," Trixie said. "And come to think of it, when the Lynches were poor and lived in a nice but rather crowded apartment on Main Street, she used to invite me home for lunch an awful lot. Her mother is a wonderful cook. I can still remember how yummy her pancakes and fried chicken tasted. Such a treat instead of sandwiches and milk!"

"Her mother doesn't cook at all any more," Honey

said. "She hardly ever goes into the kitchen."

"Why should she?" Trixie demanded. "When Di asked me to lunch last spring—that's when I saw their red trailer—the whole place was simply swarming with servants. Two nurses for the twins, if you can believe it. I wish Bobby had two nurses. He could certainly use them."

Bobby was Trixie's mischievous six-year-old brother, and more often than she liked, Trixie had to take her turn keeping an eye on him.

Honey smiled. "You *think* you'd like a lot of servants, Trixie, but you wouldn't. I was brought up by nurses, and I can tell you it's no fun."

"But the nurses don't bother Di," Trixie objected. "And the lucky duck never has to wash dishes or dust or make beds the way I do on weekends."

"Poor overworked you!" Honey's eyes twinkled with laughter. "I happen to know that Brian and Mart do most of the dishwashing at your house, and everyone but Bobby makes his own bed, and as for all that dusting—well, I've seen you do it, Trixie. A lick and a promise is the only way to describe that chore of yours. If you find a spot you can't blow off a tabletop, you put something on top of it."

Trixie chuckled. "You're right, Honey. I'd hate to have a lot of servants cluttering up our place. And nobody could possibly cook as well as Moms does. The funny part of it is, that she never makes a big fuss about it either. When she dons an apron she looks younger and prettier than ever, and she sort of wanders into the kitchen and wanders out again with an enormous meal."

"How do you know Di doesn't feel the same way about her mother?" Honey asked. "I mean, my mother can't boil water without burning it, and so she never wanders into our kitchen. The other day Miss Trask told her we needed a new spider, and Mother screamed because she thinks all spiders are black widows the way I used to." Honey giggled. "It took hours for Miss Trask to explain that the spider was a cast iron frying pan."

Trixie giggled, too. Honey's parents, grandparents, and great-grandparents had been born rich, so it didn't surprise Trixie to learn that Mrs. Wheeler was probably almost as much afraid of a frying pan as she was of a spider. Honey was most likely the first girl in the family for a long time who had cared to learn how to cook.

"What did Di say to you?" Trixie asked curiously after a moment. "I didn't realize that you two were good friends. How can you be so positive that she is unhappy?"

"She never told me she was lonely," Honey said as they started down the wide front steps of the school. "But I was a new girl when we started school, and would have been miserably lonely if it hadn't been for you, Trixie. That's how I happened to notice that Di was miserable—and yet, she isn't a new girl. Haven't you noticed? She hardly ever joins in any fun or activities and seldom speaks to the other boys and girls in our class."

Trixie said nothing. Kindhearted Honey always seemed to know when people were unhappy. Conscience-stricken, Trixie realized now that Di had changed a lot, although gradually, during the last year. She had shiny, blue-black hair that flowed around her slim shoulders, and violet eyes fringed with thick curly lashes. She was so pretty that she was always the heroine in the grade school plays although she usually got her lines and words mixed up. But nobody minded, not even the teachers, because Di always laughed when she made a mistake, and somehow managed to turn even the most serious play into a comedy.

"It's true," Trixie said suddenly. "She never laughs now, and she sort of hunches herself in a corner of the bus as though—as though she were ashamed of something. But why?"

"I don't know exactly," Honey said. "I've tried to

18

make friends with her over and over again, but every time I speak to her she looks more embarrassed than ever. See? There she is now, standing all alone at the bus stop over there. Can't we do something about her, Trixie?"

Trixie didn't have a chance to reply because they were joined then by her brothers and Jim. Brian was sixteen, a year older than Jim, but they were both juniors because Jim had skipped a grade. Brian had inherited his father's dark eyes and hair. Except that he was two inches taller, Mart looked enough like Trixie to be her twin, and they both had their mother's blue eyes and blond hair. Jim, although not related to the Wheelers, had the same red hair and green eyes that Honey's father had.

Mart was eleven months older than Trixie and often treated her as though she were Bobby's age. He was very fond of big words, too, and, because he knew it annoyed Trixie, used them frequently. He greeted his sister now with:

"Do my old eyes deceive me? Is that a notebook which you have crammed so unattractively into your skirt pocket? Am I to deduce from this evidence that you plan to spend a small portion of the forthcoming weekend in the pursuit of knowledge?"

Trixie gave him a sour look. "The answer to your

19

simple question is yes. We have to write a theme for our English class!"

Mart made a tent of his hands and rocked back and forth on his heels as though he were a lecturer on a platform. "And what, pray tell, is to be the theme of your theme?"

"None of your business," Trixie said.

"So?" Mart elevated his sandy eyebrows. "I was about to offer my services, for a small fee, a dollar to be exact. With my superior knowledge of all the subjects, my extensive vocabulary and—"

"We know, we know," Trixie interrupted. "We also know why you wear your hair in that funny-looking crew cut. Your little brain would collapse under the weight of a normal amount of hair."

"Children, children," Brian said, grinning. "Must you quarrel from morning to night? It does get a bit dull after a while."

Suddenly Honey reached out her hand and, tucking it in the crook of Di's arm, drew her into the group. "I was just thinking, Di," she said impulsively, "that it would be wonderful if you could spend the weekend with me and Jim. Here comes the bus now, but there's plenty of time for you to go back into the school and telephone your mother. You won't need any clothes. We're just about the same size, and I have loads of jeans and all kinds of T-shirts and sweaters."

Di stared at her for a moment without speaking. Then she blurted: "I don't believe it, Honey Wheeler. I don't believe you ever wear sloppy clothes. I'll bet you don't even own a pair of jeans."

"But I do," Honey said, smiling. "We all live in sloppy clothes after school and on weekends. I didn't used to own any, but last summer when I met Trixie, Miss Trask got me some so we could dress alike and have fun all the time. Miss Trask is my governess, you know."

"Your governess?" Di shook her head. "That's one thing I've been lucky enough to escape so far. How do you stand it?"

"Miss Trask isn't really a governess," Trixie put in hastily. "She runs the Wheeler place the way your butler does your place, Di. And she's a grand person. We all love her."

Di sniffed. "I can imagine! The way I love our butler. The stupid old thing! I can't even ask a few friends home for cookies and milk after school without Harrison hovering around with silver trays and fancy lace doilies. I hate him."

"Well, never mind," Honey said soothingly. "I know how you feel. We used to have butlers, too, and they were an awful bore. But now they're all gone and we have Miss Trask and Regan—"

"Who's Regan?" Di asked, and then she flushed with embarrassment. "Oh, I know I'm being nosy, and I haven't meant to eavesdrop, but I can't help hearing you kids talk on the bus. You're always shouting back and forth to each other across the aisle and I've heard you mention Regan so many times."

"He's our groom," Honey said. "We have five horses, you see, but Regan does a lot more than just take care of them. He and Miss Trask run the whole place together. I mean, the other servants take orders from them. We couldn't get along without Regan. Could we, Jim?"

Jim shook his head. The boys had been listening quietly, but now Jim said, "Make it snappy, Di. The bus will be leaving in a few minutes. Honey and I sure would like to have you spend the weekend with us. You've got just about time to telephone your mother."

Di hesitated; then she raced off.

"Oh," Trixie said in relief. "I'm awfully glad she's going to come. I thought for a minute there that she was going to say no."

Jim nodded. "She seemed pretty doubtful about the whole thing. It looked like you could use a little extra help to convince her."

"Thanks, Jim," Honey said. "It was very thoughtful

of you to invite her, too. You've all got to help me see to it that she has a good time this weekend. Di's awfully unhappy."

"She sounded pretty grim," Mart agreed. He and Brian climbed into the bus.

Jim said to Honey, "Di *is* grim. She looked desperate to me. As though she were at the end of her tether. But of course, I hardly know her. Do you know what's wrong with her, Trix?"

"I don't know," Trixie said. "She didn't used to be tense and grim."

"Well," Jim said, "I think we ought to try and find out what's making her so miserable. If for no other reason than that the motto of our club is to have a brotherly and sisterly attitude toward other kids who may need help." He climbed into the bus.

"Jim's wonderful," Trixie cried. "Most boys wouldn't have noticed that Di is unhappy. I guess he hasn't forgotten how miserable he was when he had to live with that mean old Jonesy."

"Jim is a very understanding person," Honey agreed. "That's why the boys' outdoor school he plans to start when he gets through college is going to be such a success. His pupils, even though they're orphans, won't be unhappy for one minute."

"I wish all schools were like the one Jim plans,"

24

Trixie said. "I mean, sandwiching lessons in between sports and woodcraft. Lessons are so boring."

"I wonder what's keeping Di," Honey said worriedly. "The bus will leave in another minute. I'm afraid she's going to miss it."

"Here she comes now," Trixie said. "And she's smiling for a change. So I guess all is well."

"I can come," Di said breathlessly as she climbed into the bus to sit between Honey and Trixie.

"Oh, I'm so glad," Honey cried. "You don't even have to worry about a toothbrush. Miss Trask buys them by the dozen so we always have plenty of new ones on hand for guests."

Di shook her head, the smile fading from her lips. "Mother is sending a suitcase out with our chauffeur. I begged and begged her not to, but—" She stopped, looking as though she was going to burst into tears.

"Why, what difference does it make," Trixie blurted, "whether she sends it or not?"

"I can't talk about it here on the bus," Diana whispered tensely.

"Why not?" Trixie demanded.

Di turned her face away to stare out of the window. She seemed to be very interested in the scenery.

Trixie twisted around on her seat to look out of the window, too. But there wasn't anything interesting that she could see. They were passing through the crowded section of the village and the bus had simply stopped for the light at Main Street.

Some of the boys and girls in Trixie's class who walked to and from school were standing on the corner. One of them waved to her and shouted:

"How about that English homework assignment? Tough, huh?"

"You said it," Trixie yelled back. "It's going to ruin the whole weekend."

The bus lumbered off again. Di continued to stare out of the window.

Trixie nudged her with her elbow. "What's the matter with you, Di?"

Di pretended she hadn't heard.

The other kids were making so much noise that there was no reason to whisper any longer. "Talkative, aren't you?" Trixie asked Di sarcastically.

Honey, who was sitting on the other side of Diana, shook her head, put a warning finger to her lips, and frowned at Trixie.

Trixie knew she wasn't being very tactful, but she was so curious about that suitcase that she ignored Honey. She nudged Di again. "Are you deaf, Diana Lynch? Or has the cat got your tongue?"

Di whirled away from the window then. Her violet

eyes were filled with tears and her lips were trembling. "I told you I didn't want to talk about it here on the bus," she whispered hoarsely. "Anyway, Trixie Belden, *you* wouldn't understand!"

2

A Mysterious Suitcase

THE BUS lumbered to a stop at the Beldens' driveway. Trixie and her brothers got off. "I can't figure Di Lynch out," Trixie said to Mart as Brian hurried on toward the house. "There's something mysterious about it," Trixie added, frowning.

"Oh, no," Mart moaned. "Not another mystery, Sis!"

"I don't mean that kind," Trixie said. "I don't think there's a *criminal* connected with the mystery of why she's so unhappy."

"Of course there isn't," Mart said. "She probably just imagines she's unhappy. Girls are crazy like that."

"But you didn't hear what she said about her suitcase," Trixie said, and explained. "Why should she have a fit about a simple thing like that? It just doesn't make sense to me, Mart."

Bobby, who had arrived on the grade school bus a few minutes before, appeared then. He had entered the first grade that September and was very smug about it. "Hey," he greeted them. "I know who 'scovered 'Merica. Bet you don't."

Trixie started to hoot with laughter, but Mart nudged her with his elbow and she quickly assumed a solemn expression. "Who did discover America, Bobby?" she asked.

"C'lumbus," he yelled triumphantly. Then a frown puckered his sandy eyebrows. "What's 'scover mean, Trixie?"

"Well, you know what exploring means, don't you?" she asked gravely.

He shook his blond silky curls. "You're always 'sploring, Trixie. It means going into places where you're not s'posed to go."

Mart gurgled with suppressed laughter. "That's an excellent definition of the kind of exploring Trixie does, but a more accurate definition is the word, trespassing. Isn't that right, Trixie?"

"Oh, don't confuse him," Trixie cried impatiently. "You'll just get him all mixed up with those big words.

29

Besides, the only time I ever trespassed in my life was up at the old Frayne mansion when I was trying to be helpful." She stooped to give Bobby a hug. "When Honey and I explored the mansion, what did we find, Bobby?"

"You founded Jim," he said.

"That's right," Trixie said. "But you could have said we discovered him."

"Oh." Bobby blinked his round blue eyes. "Then C'lumbus founded 'Merica?"

"Now *I'm* confused," Mart complained. "But you've got the general idea, Bobby. What else did you learn in school today?"

But Bobby had a one-track mind. "If C'lumbus founded 'Merica," he asked suspiciously, "why didn't the teacher say so?"

"Because discovered is the better word," Trixie said, beginning to lose patience. "Why don't you explore your pile of junk in the garage and see if you can discover anything worth keeping?" She straightened and said to Mart who was edging away, "In case you've forgotten, Dad said we had to clean out the garage this afternoon. He couldn't get his car inside last night."

Mart groaned. "I *had* forgotten until you brought the unpleasant subject up. Now that you mention it, I seem to recall that Fire Prevention Week looms in the immediate future. That means a scrap drive coming up soon, or am I mistaken, Trix?"

"You are so right," Trixie informed him.

"Now listen, Sis," Mart said placatingly, "you do my share. Jim, Brian, and I have to work on the club-house roof until it's time to exercise the horses. At the rate we've been going since school started, it'll be Christmas before we finish shingling it. It's Indian summer now, but we're due for rain, if not hail, snow, and sleet, around the middle of November."

Trixie merely glared at him.

"And," Mart continued, "since you are about as handy with hammer and nails as you are with thread and needles—"

"Oh, all *right!*" Trixie hated to admit it, but she knew that Mart was right. They couldn't do much about the interior of the clubhouse until the roof was finished. It was just one big room now with a dirt floor. The boys planned to partition off one end of it and line the walls in that section with shelves. Then they were going to make tables and benches for the conference room, and Honey had already bought material for curtains. They had started to work almost two months ago when the club had been formed, but their first job had been to build screens for the windows and doors. That was because Honey hated bugs, and also because when

31

they first held informal meetings without screens, they spent most of their time slapping at mosquitoes.

The tumbledown cottage was ideal for a secret clubhouse, because it had been the gatehouse of the manor in the days of carriages and sleighs, and even at this time of the year when the leaves were falling, it was almost completely hidden by ropelike vines and evergreen branches. A narrow but thickly wooded section separated it from Glen Road, and only if you knew it was there could you see it from the veranda of the big house.

All of the Bob-Whites had worked hard to earn the money for the necessary material to make the clubhouse snug and attractive. Even Jim, who had inherited half a million dollars when his miserly great-uncle died, had worked. Honey had earned her share through mending jobs, although her father, if he had known she needed money, would have given her enough so that the clubhouse would have been a little palace long ago. But one rule of the club was that every member must contribute to it money he or she had earned.

Trixie knew that she couldn't help the boys finish shingling the roof. "All right," she said again. "I'll clean the garage. You'll help me, won't you, Bobby?"

"No," Bobby said decisively. "I'm a boy. I'm gonna holp the big boys jingle the roof."

Trixie laughed. "You sound like Di Lynch when she has stage fright. I remember in one school play, when she was not much older than you, Bobby, she called Benedict Arnold, Arnold Benedict from beginning to end. Do you know who Benedict Arnold was?"

He shook his curls. "No."

Mart raced off up the driveway and into the house. Bobby started to trot after him, but Trixie grabbed his hand. "If you'll help me clean the garage, I'll tell you about Benedict Arnold. It's a very exciting story."

"Okey dokey," Bobby agreed.

"I've got to change into dungarees and an old shirt," Trixie told him. "You wait here for me on the terrace. Moms must have your orange juice ready. You can drink it with a straw and blow orange juice bubbles until I come back out again."

Trixie was only too glad to change. One thing she hadn't liked about entering junior high was that none of the girls wore jeans to school any more. Even the most tomboyish ones wore sweaters and skirts. Di Lynch, who wasn't a tomboy at all, had worn jeans until her father got rich. And this year she had started wearing dresses to school—the kind of dresses, Trixie reflected, that made her look as though she were going to a party. And on cool days when the others wore sports jackets, Di appeared in a pretty, pale blue coat that

33

made her look more than ever as though she were going to a party.

"Di has changed a lot," Trixie decided as she and Bobby started to work on the garage. "She never seems to have fun any more. Maybe it's because she's always so dressed up. Goodness knows, I can't have any fun unless I'm wearing jeans." Then she dismissed Di from her mind.

It was five o'clock by the time that Trixie, more hindered than helped by Bobby, finished cleaning the garage. Her mother joined them then, half-smiling, half-frowning.

"At least your father can get the car inside," Mrs. Belden said. "But where are the things that are to be burned or given to the scrap drive?"

"There aren't any," Trixie cried in despair. "Bobby wouldn't part with a single one of his treasures and, well, neither would I." She pointed disdainfully. "Those piles of junk there belong to Brian and Mart. I didn't dare touch their things."

"Well, run along and enjoy your ride," Mrs. Belden said. "Supper at seven."

"I forgot to tell you, Moms," Trixie said, wiping her grimy hands on the seat of her jeans. "We're all invited to dinner at the Wheelers'. Okay?"

Mrs. Belden nodded. "But you must come home first,

Trixie, and take a shower and change into at least your school clothes. You really should wear that little wool dress I bought you last spring. I'll let out the hem and press it for you."

"Oh, Moms," Trixie wailed. "I hate that silly-looking thing. And it's not a party. Mr. and Mrs. Wheeler won't be there. Besides, I won't have time to change. We're going to ride right up until dinner time. All the horses need exercise like anything."

Her father's car turned into the driveway then, and Trixie and her mother, with Bobby between them, hurried out of the garage so he could drive into it. Trixie noticed with a sinking heart that she had left her father barely enough room, and that a less skillful driver would not have been able to park without grazing at least one of the piles of junk.

Mr. Belden didn't look any too pleased as he climbed out of the Ford roadster. "I'm glad to see that there's been some sprucing up," he said. "But a lot of that stuff has to go. This place is still a disgrace and a dangerous violation of the fire laws."

"We tried to get rid of some of it," Trixie explained. "But, actually, it's all pretty valuable, Dad. There wasn't much that we could throw out."

"I holped," Bobby cried proudly.

"I'll bet you did." Mr. Belden kissed his wife and

lifted the plump little boy up to his shoulders. "Trixie," he said, giving her an affectionate pat, "I don't want to pry into your secrets, but I haven't been able to miss the fact that the boys are building some sort of a shack on the Wheeler property. If you want to keep all of that junk, I'm afraid I'll have to order you and your brothers to keep some of it in your shack."

"All right, Dad," Trixie said meekly. "I'll tell Mart and Brian about it tonight and we can move the things sometime soon."

"And," Mrs. Belden put in, "since they're dining at the Wheelers' this evening, don't you agree with me, Peter, that Trixie ought to come home first and change into a dress? I'm sure Jim and Honey don't come to the dinner table looking as though they had just cleaned a garage."

"I'm sure they don't," Mr. Belden agreed, laughing.

"But, Dad," Trixie wailed, "there won't be time between now and dinner. They're having it early so the cook and Celia can go to the early movie. And the horses have just got to be exercised today or Regan will certainly get mad at us."

"That's true," Mr. Belden said thoughtfully. "Regan is awfully good to you kids and you should be good to him. Don't let him down."

"I could take a shower in Honey's bathroom," Trixie

suggested hopefully, "and I could borrow one of her dresses. Would that be all right?"

Mrs. Belden sighed. "I guess that will be all right. But it seems to me that you are forever deciding at the last minute to spend the night with Honey and so end up borrowing her clothes."

Trixie grinned with relief. "Honey doesn't mind. She has drawers and closets full of them." She raced off along the path that led up to the Manor House. When she arrived at the stable she found that all five of the horses were saddled and bridled, but Jim and Honey were having some sort of an argument.

"Please, Jim," Honey was saying. "I'd really rather stay home. Miss Trask may have some things she would like me to do before dinner—"

Then it dawned on Trixie that if Di was going to ride, too, one of the Bob-Whites would have to drop out. And it was just like Jim and Honey to fight about which one that would be.

"I don't feel much like riding," she cried impulsively. "I'm half-dead from cleaning out the garage. You ride Susie, Di."

Diana shook her head. "I don't know how to ride. All of you please go. I don't mind being left behind. Besides, I would like to be here when my suitcase comes, so that—"

As she hesitated, flushing, Honey said quickly, "I don't want to ride, either. Lady doesn't need any exercise. Mother rode her this morning."

"Dad rode Jupe before breakfast, too," Jim added.

Regan, the pleasant-faced groom, came out of the tack room just then. "Well," he said, "the other horses do need exercise. So you Beldens had better get going before it gets so dark even the horses won't be able to see."

Trixie and her brothers quickly obeyed. Regan was usually very easygoing, but when he spoke in that tone of voice he meant business. They trotted off single file along the narrow path that led into the woods. Trixie, who was leading, said over one shoulder, "Dad knows about the clubhouse. He calls it a shack, and I don't think he knows where it is, but we've got to move a lot of our stuff that's cluttering up the garage into it. The garage just won't hold it all anymore."

"Oh, no," Mart moaned. "Why, just your junk alone, Trix, would take up so much room we couldn't hold a meeting."

"Is that so?" Trixie demanded. "What about your pup tent and those rusty old traps?"

"I use that pup tent every summer, and those traps are just as good as they ever were. If anything has to go it ought to be your——"

38

"Dad's right," Brian interrupted. "Now that I've got my driver's license, I can pack our junk in the station wagon and move it down to the clubhouse in one trip. It'll be handy to have the sleds, skis, and ice skates there. We've always done most of our winter sports at the Manor House anyway."

"True," Mart agreed. "If it doesn't rain this weekend we can finish the roof."

"And we'll move everything down there first thing. There'll be plenty of room."

Riding abreast now, they cantered across a field. Then they stopped to give the horses a rest. "I can't stop thinking about Di and her suitcase," Trixie said. "Why is she so tense about it?"

"That I don't know," Mart said. "I can't even hazard a guess. But you're right about one thing, Sis. She is very unhappy."

"I wish we could ask her to become a member of our club," Trixie said.

"I'm glad you said that." Brian smiled. "That's the way Honey and Jim feel and that's the way I feel, too. Is it okay by you, Mart?"

"Natch," Mart said. "Boy! Let's think up something terrific in the way of initiation. How about making her walk the ridgepole of the clubhouse roof? Or we could make her sleep out in the woods alone for an entire night. Or maybe we could—"

"Now, wait a minute," Trixie interrupted.

"Nothing like that," Brian said soberly. "She's so jumpy now I think we Bob-Whites ought to skip initiation in her case."

"What makes *you* think she's jumpy?" Trixie asked. "Did she do anything peculiar while I was cleaning the garage?"

"Yes and no," Brian said. "When we got off the bus, I changed my clothes and went straight up to the Wheelers'. Jim was still up in his room, so I waited for him on the porch. Di was talking to someone on the phone in the study. I tried not to listen, but I couldn't help it. She was crying and saying over and over again, 'Oh, please don't. Please don't.' "

"Well, for pete's sake!" Mart exclaimed. "What do you suppose that was all about? Didn't she try to explain?"

"She didn't see me. I stayed out on the porch, and a minute later Jim came downstairs. I guess Di went up to her room."

Trixie sighed. "She must have been talking to her mother about the suitcase. I can't see why she cares whether it arrives or not. Why should it make so much difference to her?"

"Maybe her mother was angry with her about something," Mart suggested hopefully.

"I don't think she was talking to her mother," Brian said slowly. "Because when she hung up I heard her say to herself, 'Oh, I hate him. I hate him!' "

3

A Long Lost Relative

HATE HIM?" Trixie repeated in amazement. "Why, who, I mean whom, could she have been talking to? Who could Di hate?"

"Her father, maybe?" Brian asked.

"Oh, no," Trixie cried. "Mr. Lynch is one of the kindest men who ever lived. He's big and fat in a jolly way, and so generous everyone who knows him loves him. Mrs. Lynch is darling, too. She used to be awfully jolly. The last time I saw her she was—" Trixie stopped.

"Was what?" Mart demanded.

"Kind of formal," Trixie told him. "Di invited me for lunch right after they bought that big place, and dopey me, I thought things would be just the same. So I appeared in jeans and—"

42

"—looking the way you do now," Mart finished, "as though you had just finished cleaning a garage. You probably scared the Lynches' servants. I hear they have a flock of 'em."

"Oh, stop it," Trixie cried. "I don't clean the garage *every* day."

"No," Mart admitted. "To my certain knowledge, you've never cleaned the garage before in your life. And, I gather, since Dad laid down the law about our junk, it's not what you'd call pristine right now."

"Let's stick to the subject," Brian said, giving his younger brother a light punch on the arm. "Go on, Trix. What happened at the luncheon?"

"Well," Trixie began, "it was a very elaborate luncheon, complete with the butler and a maid. Just for us three—me and Di and her mother. The twins eat in their big nursery which is in a separate wing of the house. The food was yummy but, frankly, I felt so uncomfortable I didn't enjoy it much. I guess Di knew how I felt because she never invited me again."

"Tactful you," Mart said in disgust.

"I couldn't help it," Trixie said forlornly. "I kept thinking how much more fun I would have had if I'd stayed home and eaten Moms's sandwiches and cookies."

"It's getting dark," Brian said. "We had better

remount now and start back." They trotted along in silence for a while, then he said, "It's funny, Trix. The Wheelers have pretty elaborate meals, with Celia serving in her black taffeta uniform and white apron and cap. But you never seem to feel uncomfortable at their place."

"I know," Trixie said. "I can't quite explain the difference. The Wheelers are informally formal. You know that having a lot of servants doesn't mean anything more to them than having a roof over their heads. But, Mrs. Lynch, well, I got the impression that she was scared of the butler. Harrison *is* awfully prim and proper. Oh," she interrupted herself, "maybe it was Harrison Di was talking about when she said, 'I hate him. I hate him.' "

"I doubt that," Brian said. "She may not like the butler, but I doubt if she'd cry when she talked to him over the phone."

"I've got an idea," Trixie said. "Why don't you boys go to the movies after dinner? If Di's alone with Honey and me she may tell us what's bothering her."

"That *is* an idea, Trixie," Mart said, and Brian nodded his agreement.

When they reached the stable, they groomed the horses and hurried indoors to take showers. Miss Trask stopped Trixie in the downstairs hall.

"Come into the study with me for a minute," she said. "I want to talk to you, Trixie."

"Oh, woe," Trixie thought, following Miss Trask. "What have I done now?"

Miss Trask looked puzzled. "Diana's suitcase," she began, "arrived while Regan was giving her a riding lesson on Lady in the corral. Celia was busy, so I took it upstairs to the guest room across the hall from Honey's room, and unpacked it. I'm afraid Mrs. Lynch must have got the impression that we were giving a party, for she had packed two frocks with long skirts. They're both lovely, but frankly, Trixie, I felt they were too sophisticated for a girl of thirteen." She frowned. "How long have you known Diana Lynch?"

"Since kindergarten," Trixie said. "We were very good friends until the last year or so."

Miss Trask nodded. "Judging from those frocks, I'm not sure I want Diana to become a close friend of Honey's. You see, Mrs. Wheeler doesn't want Honey to grow up too fast. We want her to be tomboy like you, Trixie, for as long as possible."

Trixie chuckled. "I'm glad somebody likes me the way I am. It seems to me that my own family has done nothing all day but lecture me on how sloppy I look."

"Everybody likes you the way you are," Miss Trask said. "You know how grateful we all are for what

45

you've done for Honey. She was a nervous, sickly child when you two met last summer. She owes Jim to you, too. Why, you're like one big happy family. I certainly don't want that to change at all."

"But why should it change?" Trixie asked.

"A newcomer to your group," Miss Trask said, "could make a difference. But perhaps I'm wrong about Diana. It's unfair to judge her when I've really only had a glimpse of her."

Then suddenly the French doors from the veranda burst open, and Di stood there, her face flaming.

She was wearing a strapless gown with a long full skirt, and she looked so grown-up that Trixie couldn't help gasping.

"I heard every word you said," she stormed, her violet eyes black with anger. "Don't you worry, Miss Trask. I'm not going to stay in this house another minute. I'll call a cab right now and leave at once."

Miss Trask was at her side in a second. "Diana, dear, I'm so sorry. I didn't know you were on the veranda. It was very wrong of me to discuss you with Trixie, but you see, she has known you for a long time, since kindergarten, really, and we—"

"Don't apologize." Di's voice was taut with suppressed tears. "Everyone likes Trixie, and nobody likes me. I shouldn't have come out here. I might have known

this would happen." She raced out of the room and up the stairs. In a minute a door slammed.

"Well, that explains a lot of things," Trixie said. "But we can't let her go home, Miss Trask. It isn't her fault that she's dressed all wrong. She didn't want her mother to send those clothes. She begged her not to. But Mrs. Lynch probably knows that Mrs. Wheeler dresses up for dinner, and so she made Di do it."

"Of course we can't let her go home." Miss Trask was already starting up the stairs. "I'll cope with this problem, Trixie."

When Trixie entered Honey's room a few minutes later, she found that Honey had just finished dressing. Trixie told her what had happened while she took a shower. "I'm beginning to see why Di is so unhappy," she finished. "I hope she doesn't go home."

"Miss Trask won't let her," Honey said as she handed Trixie clean underclothes. "Miss Trask is a very understanding person." She took a blue wool dress from one of her closets. "This ought to look nice on you, Trixie, and it won't be much too long. Not that anybody cares. But what are you going to wear on your feet? I don't think my shoes will fit you."

"My battered mocs will have to do," Trixie said. "Your feet are longer and narrower than mine, just like the rest of you is."

48

Honey giggled. "That sounds awfully ungrammatical, but I can't tell you why."

Trixie surveyed herself in the mirror. "I look like a goon, but then I always do in a dress. At least my legs are still so tanned it looks as though I were wearing stockings. Don't you think so, Honey?"

"Except for the scratches," Honey said. "But I guess they could pass as clocks."

"Clocks but no runs," Trixie said. "Come on. The suspense is killing me. If Di has gone home, what will we do, Honey?"

But Di had not gone home. They met her in the hall, and Miss Trask was with her. She was wearing a lavender wool dress that was very much like the ones Honey and Trixie were wearing.

"How nice you look," Honey said, slipping her hand through Di's arm.

The boys came out of Jim's room then, and they all trooped down to the dining room. Everyone joked and laughed a lot throughout the meal, except Di who hardly said a word. When Celia, the pretty maid, brought in the dessert, Jim said to Miss Trask, "We menfolk plan to go to the movies, but since Brian isn't allowed to drive after dark, may we ask Tom to drive us in and back?" Tom Delanoy was the Wheelers' handsome young chauffeur.

Celia blushed as she always did when Tom's name was mentioned, although everyone knew that they planned to get married some day soon.

"You'll have to ask Tom about that," Miss Trask told Jim. "It's his night off."

"I can answer for him, ma'am," Celia said, blushing more furiously than ever. "He'll be glad to do it. He can bring the boys home when he brings me back. Cook, too, if you like. But we'll—he'll need the station wagon."

"Fine." Miss Trask nodded.

When Celia went back into the kitchen, Jim said, grinning, "Tom is henpecked already. The top of Celia's head just about reaches his chin, but she's certainly going to be the boss of that family."

"That's what happens to he-men when they fall in love," Mart said, shaking his head with disapproval. "In the words of Kipling, 'The female of the species is more deadly than the male.' "

"Is that so?" Trixie demanded.

"Yes, it is so," Mart informed her airily. "Take the black widow spider—"

"Let's not and say we did," Honey interrupted with a shiver. "Which reminds me, it's Halloween next Friday. Don't you think we ought to have a party here, Miss Trask?"

Miss Trask shook her head. "I'm sorry, dear. Have you forgotten? Your mother is giving a dinner party that night."

"I know," Trixie said. "Moms and Dad are invited. So let's have the party at our house. It'll still be Indian summer, so it'll be warm enough so we can roast franks on our outdoor grill. So—"

"So, so, so-so," Mart interrupted. "How you love that word, Sis, when it isn't spelled s-e-w."

"Don't," Di cried suddenly. "Please don't."

"What?" Trixie asked in amazement.

"Don't give a party at your house." Di's cheeks were flaming and her violet eyes were filmed with tears. "You just can't give a party at your house. Mother would never forgive me."

"But I don't understand," Trixie said. "We planned to invite you, Di, if that's what you mean."

"That isn't what I mean." Di's voice was high-pitched. "*You* don't understand, Trixie Belden, because your house isn't all cluttered up with servants. When you give a party, you and your brothers do the planning and you do all the cooking, too."

"Natch," Mart said easily. "Who else?"

For answer, Di jumped up and ran out of the dining room.

"How do you like that?" Mart asked, bewildered.

51

"What did I say to make her mad?"

Jim coughed. "I think it's about time we menfolk departed."

"You're all excused," Miss Trask said, pushing back her chair.

Honey and Trixie raced upstairs to Di's room. She was lying facedown on the bed, shaking with sobs and weeping into the pillows.

"Please don't cry," Trixie begged her. "Mart didn't mean anything. What *is* wrong, Di?"

Miss Trask came quietly into the room and sat on the foot of the bed. In a soothing voice she said, "Sit up, Di, and tell the girls what you told me before dinner. Everything is going to be all right."

Di tearfully obeyed. "Mother wants to give me a Halloween party," she began. "She told me to invite all of you and the boys and girls in our class on Monday. But I didn't. I *couldn't*. Because it won't be any fun. Mother wants it to be a very elaborate affair, with Harrison hovering around like a grim ghost." She clenched her fists and rubbed her eyes with them. "I can't seem to make her understand that we don't want that kind of a party. Oh, Honey, you've got to help me."

"But how?" Honey's wide hazel eyes were filled with sympathy.

"Your mother," Di said, "is my mother's very own ideal. If your mother would tell her that it would be much better to let me give the kind of party the Beldens give, why then she would."

"It's really quite simple," Miss Trask put in. "I'm sure, Honey, that Mrs. Wheeler would like very much to invite Di's parents to the dinner she's giving next Friday night. When she telephones Mrs. Lynch tomorrow morning, she could suggest at the same time that Di's friends would have much more fun if the party Di gives is simply an informal affair."

Di nodded. "Do you think your mother would do that, Honey? I mean, explain that most of the kids will come in homemade costumes and won't like it at all if they see Harrison is hanging around in that prim way of his."

"Of course," Honey cried enthusiastically. "Harrison can be given the night off so you can run things the way you like, Di. Mother's very good about explaining things like that. She knows how *I* feel about butlers. We haven't had one since Miss Trask came to live with us. And I'm glad."

"And Regan," Miss Trask reminded her. "Regan takes the place of a butler in this household, except that he doesn't buttle."

"I wish we had a Regan on our place," Di said

enviously. "When he was giving me a riding lesson, I sort of poured my heart out to him and he was so sympathetic." Suddenly she covered her pretty face with her hands. "Oh, I forgot. *Uncle Monty!* He'll ruin everything."

"Uncle Monty?" Trixie repeated. "I didn't know you had an uncle, Di."

"I didn't," Di sobbed. "He suddenly turned up on Monday night. He's Mother's long lost brother who left home to make his fortune when she was just a baby. She has never heard from him until now."

"How exciting," Honey cried. "What on earth makes you think he'll ruin everything, Di?"

Di stared dismally up at the ceiling. "Maybe he won't. Let's not talk about him. Let's start making plans for Halloween. Maybe Uncle Monty will have gone back to Arizona by then."

"If he hasn't," Miss Trask put in, "Mrs. Wheeler will certainly invite your mother's brother to the grown-up party here that evening."

"Oh, no!" Di's voice was so high-pitched it was almost a scream. "Please, Miss Trask, don't let Mrs. Wheeler invite him out here."

Honey tactfully changed the subject to plans for the Halloween party, but Trixie couldn't help thinking: That afternoon Di Lynch had talked to someone on the

54

phone. She had sobbed: "Oh, please don't. Please don't." Then she had hung up and said to herself: "I hate him. I hate him!" Could the person Di hated so violently be her newly found Uncle Monty?

4

Trixie Is Suspicious

EXCEPT FOR special occasions, Trixie had to be home by nine o'clock, so she left right in the midst of exciting plans for the Halloween party. But her vivid imagination kept her awake and restless for a long time after she climbed into her bed.

She couldn't help thinking about Di's uncle who had suddenly turned up. In mystery stories long lost relatives who suddenly turned up always turned out to be someone else impersonating the long lost relative. What little Di had said about her uncle made Trixie feel sure that she didn't like him.

"Maybe he's an impostor," Trixie kept thinking, until she fell asleep.

As she did her chores the next morning she let her

imagination run away with her. It would be such fun to solve another mystery! If Di's uncle wasn't her mother's brother, who was he? What was he doing at the Lynches'? What was his scheme?

The practical side of Trixie's nature answered these questions coldly: Don't be silly! Just because Di doesn't like him doesn't mean he's an impostor. Besides, you don't know for sure that Di doesn't like him. And you haven't even met him yet.

By the time she had finished dusting the living room, Trixie was laughing at herself. She dismissed the mystery from her mind as she shook the dust cloth and mop out on the terrace. The sun was shining brightly but a cool breeze was blowing. It was going to be a wonderful day. Indian summer was just about the nicest time of the year, except that it happened when school was in session.

She groaned, remembering her English homework assignment. She would simply have to find time to write that theme this evening, just so she could forget about it. And she would make Brian help her. He was very good at both spelling and punctuation. Mart used a lot of big words and knew their definitions, too, but he was very apt to spell words just the way they sounded, not as they were spelled in the dictionary.

Then Trixie remembered Mart's offer to help her

write the theme—but, for a fee. "The nerve of him," Trixie said to herself as she went upstairs to make Bobby's bed. "As if I'd pay Mart or anybody else a dollar to help me!"

Bobby's bed was its usual lumpy mess which meant Trixie had to strip it. Although the little boy was only supposed to take his panda or Teddy bear to bed with him, it always seemed to Trixie as though the entire contents of his toy box were there, way down at the foot. This morning she found a water pistol, a tiny train of cars, a boat and, to her horror when she impatiently yanked off the top sheet, a whole deck of cards leaped out and flew off to every corner of the room.

"Fifty-two cards in a deck!" Trixie groaned as she stooped to get one on the floor.

But at last this chore was done, and Trixie raced out of the house. When she arrived at the Wheelers' she found the girls and Jim on the porch talking excitedly.

"Everything is wonderful," Honey told Trixie. "Mother just got through talking to Mrs. Lynch on the telephone, and Di is going to be allowed to give just the kind of a party she wants."

"Swell," Trixie said, sinking into the glider beside Jim. "With that haircut of his, Mart can go as an escaped convict. All you need to do, Honey, is whip him up a costume out of some old striped mattress

ticking. What are you going as, Jim?"

"Dracula," Jim said promptly. "It's a known fact that all vampires have red hair. I hear you're going as a goon." He nodded approvingly. "The last goon I danced with in the moonlight looked just the way you look now."

Trixie tossed her head. "Is that so? I've changed my mind. I'm going to wear the pirate's costume Mart wore at the school masquerade last year. It should fit me perfectly. All I'll need is a black wig, a red bandanna, and a big black moustache—and I'll make a cardboard knife."

"It sounds horrid," Honey said, laughing. "But a lot of fun. I think I'll go as Captain John Silver, except that I don't think I could cope with both a wooden leg and a parrot. But if Brian, our future doctor, is going as both Dr. Jekyll and Mr. Hyde, I guess I can manage. Di can't decide whether to go as Queen Elizabeth or a character out of one of Jane Austen's novels. Which do you think would look better, Trix?"

Trixie groaned. "How literary can we get? I think it would be a lot simpler if we all went in our B.W.G. shirts over our jeans, with masks and wigs. Since Di is going to become a member this weekend, there would be six of us dressed exactly alike. If we all wear the same false faces and maybe black curly wigs, we could confuse everybody and have a lot of fun."

"It's a wonderful idea," Di said thoughtfully. "Even if we don't confuse anybody but Uncle Monty. We've just got to confuse him. Otherwise I know he'll try to run things and—" She stopped and looked at Honey appealingly. "Please, you explain to Trixie and Jim."

Honey frowned. "It's hard to explain, Di, but I'll try. You see," she said to the others, "Di's afraid that even though her mother has promised to let her run the party, her uncle will interfere at the last minute and blow whistles and run around like he was a master of ceremonies on a radio or TV show."

"But why should he?" Trixie demanded. "It's not a grown-up party."

Di sighed. "You don't know Uncle Monty. He's used to running things. He was one of the first settlers in the southwest and practically made Arizona the great state it is today. Tucson would be just a ghost city if it weren't for Uncle Monty."

It was Trixie's turn to frown. "But that's not possible, Di," she said. "Last year in school when each one of us was given a state to study up on, I chose Arizona because there are so many wonderful ranches out there. You remember that, don't you?"

Di nodded. "You wrote a very interesting theme about it, Trixie, but what's your theme on Arizona got to do with my Uncle Monty?"

"Just this," Trixie said thoughtfully. "The University of Arizona, which is in Tucson, was founded in 1885. Your uncle must be an awfully old man if he had anything to do with that. And Tucson has been a boom town, for, well, just ages."

Jim nodded in agreement. "I've studied up a lot on Arizona, too, because I thought it might be the best place for my boys' school. Tucson was the territorial capital of Arizona during the ten years between 1867 and 1877. But, you see, Trixie, Arizona didn't become the forty-eighth state until 1912. Maybe Di's uncle had a lot to do with its being admitted into the Union. Maybe that's what he meant when he told her he practically made Arizona the great state that it is today."

"Maybe," Trixie admitted dubiously. "But he couldn't have been one of the first settlers. They were mostly all killed off by the Indians before the Revolution."

"He said he was one of the first settlers," Diana repeated stubbornly. "Maybe he was the only one who wasn't killed by the Indians."

Trixie laughed. "Then Uncle Monty must be almost as old as Methuselah."

"Well, he isn't," Di stormed. "He's a lot younger

than my grandfather Lynch who just had his sixtieth birthday." She glared at Trixie. "Are you trying to say that my uncle is a liar?"

"Oh, Di," Trixie pleaded. "I'm simply trying to say that he must be so old he won't want to come to your party." She chanted:

" 'On the eighteenth of April, in '75;
Hardly a man is now alive—' "

Di covered her face with her hands. "I never can remember dates, especially history dates. You're right, Trixie. My uncle *is* a liar."

"Not necessarily." Honey gently touched Di's bare arm. "I know a little something about Arizona, too, Trixie. Summer before last Daddy and Mother and I toured the whole state in our trailer. A lot of the cities that used to be ghost towns are boom towns now on account of the tourists and guest ranches. Tucson is famous for its climate. Almost too many people spend the winters out there. Di's uncle could have played an important part in the real estate boom which started not so awfully long ago. I mean, as a young man he could have bought a lot of land when it was cheap, thinking there were mines on it or something, and then, when prices skyrocketed during the years when people got the idea of building dude ranches, he could have sold it at an enormous profit."

"I guess that's what he was talking about," Diana said in a mollified tone of voice. "I didn't listen very carefully after the first hour. You know, it gets kind of stupefying when one person does all the talking."

Trixie laughed. "I can see why you're worried about your party now, Di. You're afraid your uncle will mon- mon-"

"—monopolize," Jim supplied.

"Monopolize the conversation," Trixie finished.

"But he probably has a lot of interesting stories to tell," Honey objected. "We met an old prospector in Tombstone, which used to be a ghost town, after it was first a boom town, and the stories he told for hours on end were simply fascinating. I don't think you have anything to worry about, Di."

"I'd like to meet him myself," Jim added cheerfully. "He can probably give me some pointers. A ranch in Arizona near some mountains, but with plenty of desert land for long horseback rides, might be just the place for my boys' school."

"You're going to meet him any minute," Di said forlornly. "He telephoned me here yesterday afternoon. I begged him not to, but he said he was going to drive out this morning and inspect the horses." Again she covered her face with her hands. "Oh, I wish he'd go back to Arizona and stay there. If Uncle Monty says you paid too much for Starlight and Susie, Regan will get mad, and—it's all going to be so embarrassing."

"I don't get it," Jim said wonderingly. "Why should your uncle criticize our horses?"

"That's the kind of person he is," Di moaned. "He knows everything there is to know about everything. To hear him talk you'd think he was the only bronco-buster that ever lived. He pretends to be very nice, but underneath he's really mean. When I talked to him on the phone yesterday I told him he musn't speak to Regan. I told him how important Regan is. But Uncle Monty will make him mad all right. Just wait and see."

No one said anything for several minutes. The idea of anyone criticizing Regan was almost too awful to think about. He might quit and then, because there never could be another Regan, Mr. Wheeler would certainly sell all the horses.

"He *is* mean," Di continued. "My uncle, not Regan. He keeps doing things in that sly way of his to make me miserable. Take those silly evening dresses Mother packed in my suitcase. Uncle Monty made her buy them for me just because he knew what I really wanted was some jeans. He'll think of some way to ruin my Halloween party, too. I just know he will."

"He sounds like an awfully mean person," Trixie

agreed. "And your mother is so sweet. It must be hard for you to believe that he is her brother."

Diana jumped up, her violet eyes blazing. "I see what you're driving at now, Trixie Belden! You're insinuating that my uncle is an impostor."

Trixie flushed guiltily, because, of course, she had been thinking just that. "I'm sorry, Di," she mumbled. "I was just wondering, that's all. You did say that your uncle left home when your mother was just a baby. And then he suddenly turned up on Monday night. I couldn't help sort of suspecting that maybe he isn't your real uncle. But, of course, he must have had baby pictures of her and all that kind of thing to prove that he really is."

"Of course he did," Honey said soothingly.

And then to everyone's surprise, Di suddenly whirled on Honey. "Of course he *didn't,*" she cried. "He didn't have a single solitary thing to prove that he is my mother's brother."

Trixie's mouth fell open with surprise. "Then *you* think he's an impostor, Di?"

"No, I don't," Di replied. "Because he said all the right things. He told Mother all about the night she was born—he knew the exact hour and date and where they were living then. Besides, he's been lost—if you want to call it that—for about thirty-five years, so how can you expect him to have saved anything like baby pictures of my mother even if there were any?"

"There probably weren't any," Trixie agreed cheerfully. "Babies don't go around having their pictures taken. Please forgive me, Di. I was completely wrong and I didn't mean a thing I said."

Diana smiled. "There's nothing to forgive, Trix. As a matter of fact, I wish my uncle *were* an impostor. What I really mean is, I wish he'd go away."

"Oh, oh," Trixie interrupted. "A limousine just turned into the driveway. Come on, Di. We've got to keep your uncle away from Regan. We've just got to!"

5

Di's Initiation

THE LYNCHES' big shiny limousine had turned around at the head of the driveway and was parked by the stable when Trixie, followed by Di, Honey, and Jim, got there. A small thin man, who was wearing a dark suit and light spats, climbed out from behind the wheel. He looked so dressed up for that hour of the morning that Trixie couldn't help staring at him in surprise.

Still out of breath from running, Di panted, "Hello, Uncle Monty. This is—are—Honey Wheeler and Trixie Belden and Jim Frayne."

A broad smile crinkled Mr. Wilson's weatherbeaten face. "Howdy, podners," he said. While he was shaking hands with each one, Regan appeared and was introduced. "Howdy, podner," Mr. Wilson greeted him. "I

68

take it you're the groom. Came out to give the hosses a look-see. Know quite a bit about hossflesh, if I do say so myself, podner."

"Great," Regan said pleasantly. "We bought a mare and a gelding dirt-cheap in August. I'd like to hear what you think of them."

"Oh, no, Uncle Monty," Diana cried quickly. "You mustn't take up Regan's time. He's really awfully busy today."

"Yes, that's right," Honey added. "Some other time, Mr. Wilson, when you're in riding clothes would be much, much better."

Before she had finished speaking, Jim said, "You can't judge a horse properly unless you put it through its gaits." And Trixie said:

"You must let us show you around the Wheelers' place, Mr. Wilson. It's very beautiful at this time of year when the chrysanthemums are blooming, and the dahlias, and all."

"Say, what's the matter with you kids?" Regan demanded, scratching the back of his head with a puzzled expression on his face. "Since when did you ever worry about taking up my time?"

"Why, Regan," Honey said innocently, "we always *try* to be considerate. You've often said so yourself. Why, only yesterday you told Daddy you'd quit if it weren't for the fact that we keep the horses so well exercised and groomed. Why, you're forever complaining about how overworked you are, especially in the mornings when there's so much to do. Why, I wouldn't think of letting Mr. Wilson disrupt your routine. Why—"

"That's five *whys,*" Regan interrupted. "Four too many for my money. So I'm always complaining, am I? When I do quit, and you try somebody else, see how long he lasts with five crazy kids always getting involved in mysteries, especially Trixie Belden." He gave them all, especially Trixie, a glare, and said to Mr. Wilson, "Come on inside, sir. It isn't often I get a chance to talk with an expert about horses."

As soon as the two men were out of sight, Trixie grabbed Honey's arm. "Say, what's the matter with you? You're supposed to be the tactful one. Why on earth did you have to tell Regan he's always complaining?"

"Oh, I don't know," Honey groaned. "I'm just so nervous." They moved slowly back to the porch. "Regan *is* always complaining, but he doesn't really mean it, and he's mad now because he knows *I* know he's the only groom we'd ever get to stay here and do all the things he does. Since school started we haven't exercised the horses every day, and half the time we're in such a hurry, we don't groom them properly. And—"

"Never mind, never mind," Jim said dolefully. "We know. But Regan won't quit on account of what you said, Honey."

"But he will quit," Di said in a voice that was even more doleful than Jim's, "on account of what Uncle Monty's saying right now. It's all my fault. I shouldn't have come out here in the first place. All I've done is cause everyone a lot of trouble. You'd better forget about me. I'm going to pack up my things right now and go back home with Uncle Monty."

"You'll do nothing of the kind," Honey cried, giving Di an affectionate hug. "We're all worrying about something that may never happen. I'm not an expert, but I know Starlight and Susie are fine horses. They were real bargains. Weren't they, Jim?"

Jim nodded. "Mr. Wilson and Regan are probably getting along fine. As thick as two hoss-thieves," he added with a chuckle.

Jim's young springer spaniel, Patch, and the Beldens' harum-scarum Irish setter, Reddy, came bounding up the porch steps.

Trixie greeted both dogs affectionately and said to Jim, "How are you getting on with Patch's training? When do you have time for it anyway?"

"Early in the morning and late in the evening," Jim said. "And Patch has learned a lot." Demonstrating, he said, "See? He obeys the commands, Sit, Lie, and Heel, and he's pretty good about retrieving. But Tom says he'll never point, although some springers can be taught to. The very word, springer, means to spring or flush the game. They used to be called springing spaniels, in case you didn't know."

"I didn't know," Trixie said. "I thought all spaniels and setters pointed. Reddy does, but not because anyone wants him to. Just before he dashes across Moms's flower garden after a rabbit, he sometimes lifts one paw and points his nose at it." She chuckled. "The idea is, I guess, to give Moms and the rabbit fair warning. Reddy is completely hopeless. When we tell him to sit, he lies down. When Brian and Mart tell him to heel, he goes home to his bed on the terrace. When they tell him to go home, he heels. When they tell him to lie down he runs around in circles."

Jim chuckled. "It's not Reddy's fault. The trouble with him is that all of you, including Bobby, tried to train him at the same time. I'm being very stuffy about Patch. I won't let anybody except myself, of course, give him a command—not even Honey."

"You *are* being stuffy," Honey said, smiling. "But I can see why. When the duck season opens next month, you boys will want Patch to retrieve ducks, not just any old thing he finds lying around." She turned to Trixie. "Tom's going to take them shooting in the marshes up the river, you know."

Tom Delanoy, the Wheelers' young chauffeur, was very popular with both the boys and girls. He had taught Brian and Mart everything they knew about hunting and fishing. The Beldens had recommended him for the job because, unlike many chauffeurs, Tom did not think that his work began and ended with driving the cars. He was perfectly willing to help Regan with the horses, and, in his spare time, to serve as a general handyman on the big estate. He and Regan got on very well together and shared comfortable bachelor quarters above the garage. In a way Tom, although he had been hired only a short time ago, was almost as important a member of the Wheeler household as Regan was. Regan knew everything worth knowing about horses; Tom knew everything important about cars and gun-dogs. He was full of fun, too, and very handsome with his black wavy hair and blue eyes.

"Tom likes springers all right," Jim was saying, "but his favorite breed is the pointer. If Patch were his dog, I'll bet he could train him to point. I just haven't got that much patience."

"It's your red hair," Trixie said, grinning.

73

Di, who had been sitting forlornly on the edge of the glider, said, "Oh, let's not talk about red hair. It reminds me of Regan and what Uncle Monty may be saying to him right now."

Jim quickly changed the subject. "Where are Brian and Mart, Trixie? It's getting on to the time we set for initiating Di into our club."

"They'll be here pretty soon," Trixie told him. "They have to stack all of our junk that's in the garage into the station wagon. Then Brian's going to drive it to the clubhouse. Maybe they're down at the clubhouse now waiting for us."

"Let's go," Jim said, leading the way down the sloping lawn to the cottage.

"What's my initiation going to be like?" Di asked nervously. "I'm sort of scared."

"I don't know," Trixie said. "Honey and I left it up to the boys. What does Di have to do, Jim, to become a member of our club?"

Jim shrugged. "I left it up to Brian and Mart. We talked about it on the way home from the movies last night, but I couldn't think of a thing. Except," he added to Di, "make you try to eat a dozen eggs in as many minutes. How would you like that?"

"Ugh," Honey gulped. "I was in a pie-eating contest at boarding school last year. The girl who won ate five blueberry pies in only thirty minutes. She was awfully sick afterwards."

"I don't like to eat either eggs or blueberry pie," Di wailed.

"Never mind," Trixie said. "If my brothers have anything to do with it, it won't be that kind of initiation. Mart will probably make you walk barefooted on a mile of tacks. Or make you try to put up his pup tent all by yourself. That's the kind of torturer he is."

Di shuddered, and Honey quickly tucked her hand through the crook of Di's arm. "Don't pay any attention to Trixie," Honey said. "Mart is an awful tease, but he's really very kindhearted."

When they arrived at the cottage they found that Brian and Mart were already there, neatly stacking the winter sports equipment they had brought from home. To Trixie's surprise and dismay, Bobby was there, too, "holping," as he proudly told them.

Trixie put her thumbs in her ears, waggled her fingers, crossed her eyes, and stuck out her tongue. "Do we *have* to have you-know-who here in our clubhouse?" she asked Mart sourly.

"Whom," Mart corrected her. "And we do, unless you want to go home and play in the sandpile with whom." He moved closer and peered intently at Trixie's face. "Some day your eyes are going to stay crossed,

Sis. And your thumbs will stay in your ears and your tongue will be permanently stuck out. But I wouldn't worry if I were you, Sis. Somehow, you look better that way. And think of the money you'll save. You won't need a mask for Halloween. Not that you really do anyway, with the funny face you were born with!"

"Oh, is that so?" Trixie demanded. "Have you forgotten that we are supposed to look exactly alike except for that weird haircut of yours? And in case you're interested, I do not have to stay home and play with you-know-whom today. Moms said that after I did the dishes and the dusting I could have the rest of the day off. She canned the last of the tomatoes yesterday, so—"

"True," Mart interrupted, "but because of which, our paternal parent feels that our maternal parent needs a vacation." Holding his thumb and index finger to one eye in the form of a monocle, he said with a very pronounced British accent, "The pater and mater have gone off on a motaw trip, old thing. Thus we are saddled with the younger generation until evening, or at least until late afternoon."

"We!" Trixie sniffed. "You mean you and Brian are. And, in case you're interested, you've ruined everything. How can we initiate Di with Bob—I mean, you-know-whom in our hair?"

"In case *you're* interested," Mart said airily, "that is what the initiation ceremony is going to consist of. We thought of blindfolding her and making her walk a plank into the lake. We even went so far, in our fiendish way, of planning that she should pound her thumbs to a pulp while we supervised her as she finished shingling the roof. Then it came to us. What better opportunity could she have of proving that she is worthy of being a member of the brotherly and sisterly secret society known as B.W.G.'s than by coping all the rest of the day, alone and absolutely unassisted, with the devil incarnate in the form of young Robert Belden, Esquire?"

Trixie, convulsed with laughter, collapsed on the sled Brian had just brought in. The three older boys joined in her laughter. Honey smiled rather nervously, but Di stood at the entrance to the cottage looking completely bewildered. She looked from Trixie to the boys to Honey and back to Trixie again.

"I—I don't understand what you're talking about," she said after a while. "I know you can't join any secret club without being initiated in one way or another, but what will I—"

Honey threw one arm around Di's shoulder. "It couldn't be simpler, Di," she said. "All you have to do is keep Bobby amused, and he's really a little angel in spite of what Mart said. He can sail boats in the wading pool up near the house, and Regan will give him a riding lesson on Lady about eleven, then it'll be time to clean up for lunch, and then after lunch he has a long nap—"

"Not forgetting the comics," Trixie interrupted. "He suffers from insomnia in the daytime, Di, which means you have to read *Peter Rabbit* to him over and over again. And as for Regan and the riding lesson, how do you know Regan hasn't already quit?"

"Regan—quit?" Brian and Mart almost shouted in one quick breath.

Trixie explained while her older brothers listened in horrified silence. "Of course," she finished, "we're not absolutely certain that Mr. Wilson will insult Regan. But if he says anything at all that gets Regan's goat—well, I guess I don't have to tell you what will happen." She shrugged.

"Please don't go into the ghastly details," Mart moaned. "If Regan quits, it's the end of everything." He turned to Honey. "If that happened, your dad would get rid of the horses, wouldn't he?"

Honey was nervously clasping and unclasping her slim hands. "Oh, I don't know what Daddy would do. He and Regan both have red hair, you know, and the quick tempers that go with it. Although Daddy thinks the world of Regan, I don't think he'd exactly get down on his hands and knees and beg him to stay if Regan decided to quit right now and started to leave in a huff."

Jim nodded in full agreement. "And we all know that we'd never find another groom who would put up with us kids. But," he added, "we're probably making a mountain out of a molehill. In spite of what you blondes and brunettes think, redheaded people don't fly off the handle all the time. Take me, for instance." He grinned. "Why, I'm just about the sweetest-tempered boy in the whole wide world!"

"Is that so?" Trixie demanded with a sniff. "How about that time last summer when you jumped down my throat simply because I implied that you were not telling the truth?"

"You know I was telling the truth that time, Trix," Jim insisted, starting to get angry.

"Sweet-tempered Jim," Trixie chanted and everyone laughed.

"Don't mind us, Jim," Honey said at last, "we're just trying to tease you. Besides, we've got another temper to worry about right now. Do you think there's a chance Uncle Monty won't say anything insulting to Regan?" Honey asked Di.

"You don't know Uncle Monty," Diana answered.

"He's sure to insult Regan somehow. He's one of those people who knows all the answers. Why, last night he told Dad that our house slowly but surely was being eaten alive by termites."

Brian laughed, but there wasn't the slightest sign of a smile in his black eyes. "Is it possible, Di," he asked, "that your uncle is an exaggerator?"

"It's worse than that," Diana said, gulping. "He's a liar, that's what he is. Uncle Monty lies all the time. I know it. *I know it!*"

"Oh, Di," Honey cried. "You mustn't talk that way about your mother's own brother. A lot of people exaggerate. Trixie and I do all the time, but it doesn't mean that we're liars."

"Uncle Monty is, though," Diana insisted. "He told us that he made a lot of money but he lost it all because he's been sick for the past ten years. But if you could see him eat, you'd know that he's as healthy as an ox. I think he just pretends to be sick so he won't have to work, and that means he'll live with us for the rest of his life. If you want my candied opinion—"

"The word is can*did*," Mart interrupted and was promptly silenced by Brian who gave him a brotherly punch and said sternly:

"Keep your outsize vocabulary to yourself, bud. Go on, Di."

But it was too late. Di wordlessly shook her head, wheeled stiffly, then broke into a run. The Bob-Whites helplessly watched her as she raced across the lawn and up the steps to the big house.

6

Halloween Plans

Now YOU'VE done it," Trixie cried, giving Mart a disgusted look. "Di is sure to pack up and go home."

"I'm sorry," Mart said shamefacedly. "I was just trying to be funny. I mean, she gets so tense about everything I thought if she laughed she might relax."

"She is tense," Honey agreed, "but it's just because she hasn't had any fun for a long time, Mart. When you're unhappy you don't have a sense of humor. I'm going up to her room now and try to talk her into staying."

Brian nodded. "We'd better skip initiation in her case. Trixie, you go up to the garage and check on Regan. Take Bobby with you. If Regan is mad, Bobby will be a big help. He adores the kid."

Bobby, who hadn't been listening to their conversation until now, grinned and took Trixie's hand. "Regan 'dores me," he said smugly. "And I 'dore Regan. He *never* gets mad at me."

The girls started off with Bobby between them. When they reached the steps they saw that the Lynches' limousine was moving down the driveway. Mr. Wilson was alone in the front and he was staring curiously at the house. There was no one in the back seat.

"Well, Di's still here anyway," Honey said. "Trixie, we've got to be awfully careful of what we say to her. She's very sensitive about her mother and her uncle. Let's keep the conversation away from them. Even if Mr. Wilson isn't quite honest we ought not to talk about it in front of Di!"

"Okay," Trixie agreed. She and Bobby hurried on to the stable and found Regan in the tack room cleaning a saddle. "Hello, Regan," Trixie said nervously. "How are you?"

He dropped the sponge and placed both hands on his hips as he stared down at her. "What goes on here anyway?" he demanded. Then he scooped the little boy into his arms. "Is your sister nuts or something?" he asked Bobby. " 'How am I?' she asks, a question she never asked me before in her whole life. A lot she cares how I am. And it's plain to be seen that I never felt better. Do I look sick?" he asked Trixie.

"No," Trixie said, flushing. "But I just wanted to know. You're not mad at anybody, are you?"

He narrowed his eyes suspiciously. "Should I be? Don't bother to answer. I should be, but I haven't found out why yet. *What have you kids been up to?*"

"Nothing," Trixie replied hastily. Then because her curiosity got the better of her, she blurted: "How did you get on with Mr. Wilson?"

Regan guffawed. "Why, just fine. He's a nice little man, but what he doesn't know about horses would fill the Sleepyside Public Library."

"But, Regan," Trixie cried, "he used to be a bronco-buster. He must know a lot about horses."

Regan laughed so hard that he had to set Bobby down on the floor in order to wipe his streaming eyes. "Broncobuster! Unless I miss my guess, that guy's never been on a horse in all his life."

"But he said—" Trixie began and interrupted herself. "I can't understand this. Why did he come out here posing as an expert?"

"That I can't tell you," Regan said. "Unless he thought he could fool me. He's been reading up on the subject all right. Uses words like spavin and fet-lock correctly. Good grooms are scarce, in case you don't know it. A lot of rich people have to hire guys who don't know much more than Mr. Wilson. But if you've spent most of your life with horses, as I have, you can see through that kind of bluff right away."

"Does he know you saw through him?" Trixie asked thoughtfully.

"Certainly not," Regan replied emphatically. "Would that have been polite of me? He's the pretty little girl's uncle, isn't he?"

"I'm not so sure that he is," Trixie said, thinking out loud. Then remembering that "little pitchers have big ears," she said to Bobby, "Why don't you go to the garage and see what Tom Delanoy is doing? You haven't seen him in ages."

"Don't want to," Bobby said, squeezing Regan's soapy sponge with both plump hands. "I'm going to stay here and holp Regan."

"Not today you aren't," Regan said firmly. "You go next door and 'holp' Tom. He's washing the cars. That's more fun than cleaning leather."

"Okey dokey," Bobby said, and scampered off toward the garage.

As soon as he was out of earshot, Regan said to Trixie: "Now listen, if you're off on one of your mysteries again, let me warn you. Nice people like that Lynch girl don't have uncles who are crooks. Mr. Wilson is just one of those harmless little guys who likes

to hear himself talk. Eccentric, you might call him, but aren't we all? You and your brother Mart, for instance, are as crazy as June bugs, and do you think anyone in his right mind would stick around here as long as I have? Ever since you arrived on the scene, they should have changed the name from the Manor House to the Madhouse!"

Trixie giggled. "I guess you're right. The trouble with me is that I have a suspicious nature."

"That you have," Regan said, grinning. "I got to know Di Lynch pretty well yesterday when I was giving her a riding lesson. She's got enough troubles without you sleuthing around after her uncle. Right now you think he's an impostor, don't you?" he finished abruptly.

Trixie nodded.

"Well, leave that up to Mr. Lynch," Regan said sternly. "He's no fool. Nobody who could make a million dollars as fast as he did could be."

"I guess you're right," Trixie said again. "I was just thinking—"

"Don't," Regan interrupted. "Don't think. Every time you do, this place is swarming with state troopers and G-men."

Just then Di and Honey came into the tack room, arm-in-arm. Honey gave Trixie a quick, questioning look and asked, "How are you, Regan?"

At that the groom emitted a loud groan and stalked away.

"Oh, dear," Honey sighed. "Uncle Monty did make Regan mad, didn't he, Trixie?"

"No," Trixie said. "Everything is just fine. He's crazy about your uncle, Di."

"I don't believe it," Di said in amazement. "Nobody could be crazy about Uncle Monty. Oh, Mother loves him, of course, but what I mean is—a man like Regan! You just can't make me believe you, Trixie Belden. Regan couldn't possibly even *like* Uncle Monty."

Trixie said nothing as the girls linked arms and strolled back up to the veranda. To change the subject, tactful Honey said:

"We've got an awful lot to do this weekend, Di. We've not only got to make plans for your Halloween party, but we've got to write those compositions for our English class. What are you going to say in your theme, Di?"

"I haven't given it much thought," Diana admitted. "We didn't do anything exciting last summer."

"Why, Di!" Honey cried. "It was your red trailer that disappeared so mysteriously. I'd certainly call that incident exciting!"

"I know," Di said. "But you and Trixie will tell

about that. I didn't have a thing to do with solving the mystery."

"Don't be silly," Trixie said generously. "That story is yours, all yours. If you haven't got the newspaper clippings, Honey and I will be glad to lend you our scrapbooks, won't we, Honey?"

"Do you really mean it?" Di asked incredulously.

"Of course we mean it," Honey said as they settled down in the glider. "Trixie and I have so much to write about we hardly know where to begin. Let's do our themes right now while we're all together. It'll be fun!"

"Not with Bobby in our hair," Trixie objected. "Every time we try to put two words together into a sentence, he'll interrupt. I know that fiend. You never can find him when you want to give him a bath or put him to bed. But just try to hide from him! He's got the nose of a bird dog, or maybe I mean a bloodhound."

Diana giggled and Trixie could see that she was beginning to relax. "I'll go play hide-n'-seek with Bobby right now," she offered. "Then you girls can write your themes in peace. I wouldn't want to borrow your scrapbook," she said to Honey, "until you're through with it. I'm sure it must be filled with newspaper clippings which you and Trixie will need."

The rest of the weekend everything went smoothly. Di insisted upon taking care of Bobby as her initiation, and Honey kept her company most of Saturday while she made Diana a red jacket like the others with B.W.G. cross-stitched in white on the back. By Sunday evening they had invited everyone on the list to the Halloween party, and were completing plans for it.

"M-m-m, let's see," said Honey, who, as secretary of the club, had been checking off names on the list. "Twelve girls and fifteen boys. That means about ten pounds of chopped meat for hamburgers, at least six dozen frankfurters, about a gross of rolls, several gallons of ice cream, a couple of cases of soft drinks, and milk for those who don't want Cokes. And we musn't forget mustard, relish, catsup, and butter. You ought to order all of this stuff from the store right after school tomorrow, Di, and make sure that it's delivered Friday afternoon."

"What are you going to do with it after it arrives?" Trixie asked. "Practically all of it should go right into the refrigerator. Is your mother's refrigerator large enough for all the food, Di?"

"We've got two huge ones and a gigantic freezer," Di said, "but they're always crammed full. I'm beginning to see what Mother meant when she said we ought to hire caterers. What am I going to do, Honey?"

Honey chewed her pencil worriedly. "We can't ask your mother's advice now when she has said you can run the party yourself. We've got to cope with the problem, but I don't see how." She thought for a minute. "We don't really have to serve milk, and you can buy the ice cream packed in dry ice."

"And," Trixie added, "you can buy a big chunk of ice for the soft drinks. We always do, and we keep it in a tub. Frozen hamburger doesn't have to be kept in a refrigerator, and neither do canned frankfurters. If the butter's soft it'll be that much easier to spread."

"How smart you are," Di said admiringly. "If we get the things you suggested, we won't have to go near the kitchen. I'll just have everything carried onto the terrace as soon as it's delivered."

"Suppose it rains?" Honey asked dubiously. "This heat wave we've been having is bound to end in a thunderstorm soon."

"That won't matter," Di said. "Our terrace is enclosed. It's really more of an outdoor living room which runs all along one side of the house. We can cook the food on the big fireplaces at each end of it."

"Marshmallows," Trixie yelled. "Halloween wouldn't be Halloween without toasted marshmallows."

"And popcorn," Diana added. "We forgot all about that important item."

"I'm beginning to get nervous," Honey said, chewing her pencil again. "We've probably forgotten all sorts of important things. I think we should add to the list paper plates and napkins and straws. If we cause the servants a lot of extra work, Di, Harrison will raise a fuss and then your mother may not let you attempt to give another party by yourself."

"I wish he'd get mad enough to quit," Di said crossly. "The way he acts, you'd think he owned our place. I hardly ever see my little brothers and sisters because Harrison doesn't like children that age. He's afraid they'll break something in the living room or put their sticky hands on the slipcovers, so the twins spend most of their time in the nursery when they're not outdoors." She turned to Trixie. "You may not believe me, but I had fun taking care of Bobby yesterday. You don't know how lucky you are to have a little brother you can hug and kiss whenever you feel like it."

"Oh, I know," Trixie said sympathetically. "Bobby is an awful nuisance sometimes, but he really is so cute. And I have no business complaining when I have to take care of him. Moms always pays me twenty-five cents an hour when I do, and I get an allowance of a dollar a week, too." She added shamefacedly, "You're right, Di, I guess I am a pretty lucky girl."

"That reminds me," Di said worriedly. "How am I going to earn some money so that I can contribute to

93

the club like you both did?"

"Let's not worry about that now," Honey said quickly. "Your party is the most important thing. If it's a success without Harrison having anything to do with it, maybe your mother will decide you don't need a butler."

"Maybe," Di said without much hope. She peered over Honey's shoulder at the list. "We've forgotten about prizes. What games do you think we ought to play?"

"Oh, I know a wonderful game," Trixie cried. *"Murder at Midnight!* It's more fun."

Di shuddered. "It sounds delightful. I'm beginning to think you *are* a goon, Trixie. Or should I have said, ghoul?"

Trixie laughed. "To win a prize in this game, you can't be either a goon or a ghoul. You've got to have brains. There are all sorts of ways of playing *Murder at Midnight,* but this is the way we play it at our parties. First you deal out cards. The person who gets the Queen of Spades is the murder victim. The person who gets the Ace of Diamonds is the murderer. But, of course, he doesn't let anybody know that. Then you choose up sides. Half of the gang goes out of the room with the Queen and the Ace. The murderer tells his side who he is and they leave all sorts of clues around, trying to baffle the other side. The person who is smart enough to guess who the murderer is gets first prize."

Honey giggled. "Who gets the booby prize? The Queen of Spades?"

"No," Trixie told her. "The 'detective' who asks stupid questions and sort of blunders around. There's always somebody like that at every party."

"I'm going to give myself the booby prize right now," Diana said, smiling. "But that game does sound like fun, Trixie, and our house is so big it'll take practically all evening to find the clues and solve the mystery."

"You can't tell," Honey argued. "At every party there's always somebody who's awfully smart, too. He or she might solve the mystery very quickly. To be on the safe side we really ought to think up some more games. Got any more ideas, Trixie?"

"Well, there's that relay of passing a paper bag and having each one in line eating whatever wrapped article he or she grabs on to," Trixie said thoughtfully.

"That sounds good," laughed Diana.

"Or how about bobbing for apples?" Trixie asked. "It's the thing to do on Halloween, isn't it?"

"No," Di said emphatically. "*You* don't mind getting your hair wet because it's naturally curly, but a lot of girls wouldn't like it."

95

"Personally," Honey said, "I think we're all too old for that kind of game. After *Murder at Midnight*, if there's time, I think we ought to play guessing games. You know. A group acts out a line from Shakespeare or something and the others have to guess what they're trying to say."

"Okay," Trixie agreed. "Charades are always fun. Not that I'd know a line from Shakespeare from a straight line somebody drew with a ruler."

"Oh, stop it," Honey protested. "You get very high marks in English, Trixie. Why must you always go around acting as though you were illiterate? I think the theme you wrote yesterday was just wonderful, and I'll bet the teacher thinks so, too."

"*If* she can read my horrible handwriting," Trixie said with a rueful grin. "And that gives me an idea for another game. We can analyze one another's handwriting. Mart's got a book on the subject. If things get dull we can always make a fortune-teller out of him. He'd love it."

All week when the girls met at school or on the bus they added to the list, but in the end it wouldn't have mattered if they hadn't made any plans at all.

The Bob-Whites, as assistant hosts and hostesses, were the first guests to arrive at the party.

Diana greeted them tearfully. "It's all happened just

96

the way I told you it would. And he did it on purpose just to be mean. I know he did."

"Who did what?" Trixie asked in amazement. "Don't tell me Harrison didn't take the night off after all?"

"He's still here, too," Di said exasperatedly. "But I told him flatly he couldn't answer the door. But I'm not talking about him. I'm talking about Uncle Monty. He's running everything, and it's all such a mess that I don't know what to do!"

7

Lots of Surprises

SURE ENOUGH, Uncle Monty *was* running everything. As a "surprise" for Diana, he had persuaded Mrs. Lynch to order caterers, a five-piece orchestra, and even decorators from New York. The walls of the downstairs rooms were draped in black sateen on which weird, luminescent shapes had been painted. Witches, cats with huge fangs and arched backs, pumpkins and spiders—all done in luminous paint—grinned eerily down from the black drapes hanging near the entrance.

"Wow, just look at these decorations," Brian said.

"It certainly looks like a Halloween party, doesn't it, Trixie?" Jim said.

"It looks like something out of a movie," Trixie

gasped, trying to see it all at once.

"That's just it," Diana wailed. "Hollywood! And I planned that everything would be so nice and simple." She led them into the long room which was called the art gallery. You couldn't see any of the pictures now because of the ghostly draperies, and the carpet and all of the furniture had been moved to the terrace. The orchestra was tuning up on a raised platform at one end, and the folding doors at the other end of the room were closed.

"Even if they were open," Di said, "you couldn't get out on the terrace it's so packed with furniture. And I guess they've thrown out all the stuff I ordered. Wait till you see the dining room. The table is positively groaning under turkeys and hams and all sorts of fancy appetizers. And it looks to me as though there must be a waiter for every guest."

"Never mind, Di," Honey said soothingly. "Everyone's going to have a wonderful time."

"That's right, just wait and see, Di," Trixie said, and the boys heartily agreed.

"But what are we going to do?" Di demanded. "A lot of the kids who are coming don't know how to dance. I don't myself. But you can't get that through Uncle Monty's head. He has made up his mind that we're going to spend the whole evening dancing and eating.

How are we going to play the games we planned with the orchestra making so much noise and all the rooms cluttered up with waiters and fancy decorations?"

Honey smiled. "The caterers won't bother us, Di. They'll serve supper, then clean up everything and go back to New York. And if nobody wants to dance, why the orchestra can leave then, too. Your mother is still here, isn't she? Couldn't you ask her if that would be all right? I'm sure she'd say it was."

Diana shook her head. "You don't understand. I c-can't explain."

"I understand," Trixie cried impulsively. "You don't want to hurt your mother's feelings. She thought you'd be pleased with these arrangements."

"That's right," Di said, her cheeks flaming. "She let Uncle Monty talk her into thinking all of this would be a grand surprise. Dad is perfectly furious, because he knows how I feel. I mean, he's awfully mad at Uncle Monty. If you want my candied—I mean, my candid opinion, Dad can't stand the sight of Uncle Monty. That's what I was trying to tell you all on Saturday when I got all mixed up and acted so babyish. I think Dad would give Uncle Monty all of his money if it meant that Uncle Monty would go away and stay away." Di crammed her clenched fists into the pockets of her red B.W.G. jacket. "Oh, I wish he would. I hate

Dad's money almost as much as I do Uncle Monty."
She ran out of the room.

Honey shook her head. "I think Di's uncle was mean
to ruin her plans, but she shouldn't hate her mother's
brother."

"I understand how she feels," Jim said sympathetically. "I hated my own stepfather. Remember,
Honey?"

"That was different," Honey said. "Jonesy was, well,
a beast. And he wasn't a blood relative. He wasn't any
more related to you than David Copperfield was to
that awful Mr. Murdstone his mother married. But
David's great aunt Betsy Trotwood, who didn't sound
very nice in the beginning of the book, was a blood
relative, and—well, you've all read *David Copperfield* so you know what I mean."

"You mean that blood is thicker than water," Brian
said soberly. "And it is. Usually."

Mart chuckled. "True, true. We have an aunt named
Alicia who keeps on thinking that Trix will become a
lady some day and manage to handle a needle as though
it were not a crowbar. Aunt Alicia even went so far
as to try to teach our sister to tat once, but Trix doesn't
hate her, do you Trix?"

"Brown eyes," Trixie said suddenly.

They all stared at her in amazement.

101

"Well, he has got brown eyes," Trixie said defensively. "Mr. Wilson has. And Mrs. Lynch's eyes are as blue as blue delphiniums."

"So what?" Brian demanded. "You and Mart and Bobby have Moms's blue eyes, and mine are black like Dad's. Does that prove that I am an adopted child?"

"No one in his right mind would have adopted you," Trixie said with a sniff. "I wasn't trying to prove anything. I was just thinking out loud as usual." Suddenly she remembered what Regan had said: "Don't think." And what Honey had said:

"Even if Mr. Wilson isn't quite honest, I don't think we ought to talk about it in front of Di."

She opened her mouth to change the subject, but Jim was saying cheerfully, "Speaking of adopted children, I'm one and my eyes are neither black nor blue. They're green. What does that make me, Trix?"

At that moment Di and her uncle joined them at the entrance to the gallery. Mr. Wilson was dressed as a cowboy complete with chaps and toy pistols, and looked to Trixie rather like a wizened little boy. Rubbing his hands together gleefully he said, "On with your wigs and masks, podners. The other guests will be arriving soon. I've got it all arranged. No unmasking until the bell rings for chow. Soon as everyone gets here, we'll have a grand march around the ballroom,

with me as judge. First prize goes to the best costume. Booby prize goes to the worst. Then we'll do some square dancing, podners, until we work up an appetite for grub. I'll do the calling. There's not much old Uncle Monty doesn't know about square dancing. Why, if I had my fiddle here, I'd play 'Turkey in the Straw' as you never heard it before. If I had my accordion and mouth organ here, I'd show all of the guests what a real one-man orchestra was like. Music right out of the West!"

"I'm sure you would, Uncle Monty," Di said, forcing a smile to her taut lips. "But since almost none of the boys and girls I've invited knows how to dance, I thought we might let the orchestra leave when the caterers go. Is that all right?"

"Oh, no, no, no, NO!" her diminutive uncle cried, hopping up and down with each "No" as though he were the dwarf, Rumpelstiltskin. "If your guests can't dance there are plenty of games we can play to music. Musical chairs, London Bridge Is Falling Down, and all that sort of thing."

"But, Uncle Monty," Di cried, "we're too old for that kind of game."

"Then you're old enough to waltz and do the two-step and the polka," he said firmly. The orchestra struck up the "Blue Danube" and he bowed gallantly in front

104

of Honey. "This little lady can waltz, I'll betcha. May I have this dance, miss?"

Trixie held her breath. Now was the time for Honey to be her most tactful self! And Honey was. She dropped a curtsy and said sweetly: "I'd rather not, Mr. Wilson, but I do think your idea of keeping the orchestra on is just great. With you as master of ceremonies, we could have a real quiz show. The orchestra can play a few bars of a song, and the one who names the song first gets a prize." She laid a slim hand on the decorated cuff of his sleeve. "Why don't you and I go into Mr. Lynch's study and make a list of the songs we think the orchestra ought to play for that contest?"

He followed her out of the gallery and into the room across the hall as meekly as a lamb. Trixie let out her breath in a long sigh. "That's the answer, of course," she said. "From now on we've all got to take turns keeping Uncle Monty from being an emcee."

The boys nodded solemnly, and Di said gratefully, "Oh, will you? I can't help because I'm the hostess." The front door bell rang then and she hurried off, completely forgetting to don her false face and wig in her eagerness to greet the guests before her uncle did.

Without saying a word, the Beldens and Jim took their wigs and masks from the pockets of their jackets and put them on. They all looked very funny, but nobody laughed. For a moment Trixie felt dizzy. In their shapeless jackets, black curly wigs and realistic, rubber devil's faces, it was impossible to tell the boys apart. Mart wasn't, of course, quite as tall as Brian and Jim, but somehow they all seemed now to be exactly the same height. They stood there, as motionless as the luminescent ghosts, witches, skeletons, and dragons on the black draperies. It was hard to breathe behind the close-fitting mask, and for the first time in her life Trixie felt weak and wobbly-kneed, as though she might faint at any moment.

The folding doors at this end of the gallery had been pushed back as far as they would go. Trixie grabbed one of the brass handles to steady herself, and something big and black and horrible with skinny, wiggly legs sprang at her. It dropped on her out-stretched hand, then slithered to the floor at her feet.

8

Hidden Portraits

IT WAS a black widow spider! But, Trixie realized, as she stifled the scream in her throat, far too large to be real. Thinking that one of the boys had played the trick on her, Trixie said over her shoulder:

"Very funny. Very funny. You'd better not scare Honey with spiders. She has a phobia about them."

Then she heard Jim's voice, cold with anger. "It wasn't funny at all. That kind of practical joke can be downright dangerous. You didn't have anything to do with it, did you, Brian and Mart?"

Both the Belden boys shook their heads and said, "No," in unison.

"It's probably Uncle Monty's idea of fun," Mart said, and Trixie could tell that he was even angrier than

Jim was. "I don't like that guy." He tucked Trixie's cold hand protectively through the crook of his arm. "Anybody but you would have screamed, fainted, or gotten hysterical."

Brian gave Trixie's free hand a brotherly squeeze. "For two cents," he said, "I'd say we all might just as well go home. It's not going to be any fun taking turns keeping Uncle Monty out of everybody's hair. I don't dislike him personally, but he's certainly doing his best to make Di miserable."

Jim, who had been examining the handle on the folding door, straightened. "I see how the contraption works. A rubber band and a thumbtack is the secret. I'm darned glad it wasn't Honey who grabbed that handle, Trixie. She's just beginning to get over her fear of spiders. Something like this would have been a serious setback. I wonder how many more booby traps Uncle Monty's set around the place."

"Ah, the place is probably crawling with them," Mart said disgustedly. "As I said before and I'll say again, I don't like that guy."

"Neither do I," Trixie agreed. "I'm sure he's an impostor."

"Now, Trix," Brian said cautiously, "just because he's different from other people and sort of eccentric in his ways and has a warped sense of humor—"

"It's not that," Trixie interrupted. "He doesn't look anything like Mrs. Lynch. She's so plump and pretty and really quite tall, with those blue, blue eyes. And he's so shriveled and little with eyes that always make me think of olive pits."

"That doesn't mean a thing," Mart pointed out. "Aunt Alicia doesn't look a thing like Moms, and yet they're sisters."

"Yes," Trixie said, "but we know that Aunt Alicia looks like our grandfather and Moms looks like our grandmother. If we knew that Mrs. Lynch's parents both had blue eyes we'd know for sure that Uncle Monty was an impostor."

Brian whistled. "You've got something there. Blue is recessive, so blue-eyed parents can't have a brown-eyed child."

"It's the Mendelian theory of heredity," Trixie said. "Moms told me all about genes and things when we were working in the garden last summer. She's crazy about the subject of dominant colors on account of flower seeds, you know. It's why her flowers almost always win prizes at the Garden Club shows."

"It's an interesting subject," Jim said, "but as I recall, Mrs. Lynch's parents died when she was a baby, so how will you ever find out whether or not they both had blue eyes?"

"That's right," Mart said. "Now, take me for instance. I have a fabulous memory, but I can't remember a thing that happened to me when I was a babe in arms. In fact, my earliest recollection is my third birthday party when Trix fell into my cake. My mental picture of her at that time is not that her eyes were blue, but that her eyelashes were plastered with pink frosting."

Trixie sniffed. *"My* earliest recollection is your fourth birthday party when you scorched your eyelashes trying to blow out all the candles on your cake at once."

"Children, children," Brian admonished them. "Can't you let bygones be bygones?"

"If Mart would stop interrupting," Trixie complained, "I have something important to say."

Mart snapped his fingers over her head. "Speak, girl, but bark, don't growl."

Trixie took a deep breath. "Last spring, as I've already told you, Di invited me out here for lunch. It was all very elaborate with everything from soup to nuts, Jim, and I didn't have much fun. I realize now that Di didn't either, but—"

"You know what?" Jim interrupted thoughtfully. "Di has a phobia about being rich. We've got to cure her of it, just as we have almost cured Honey of her phobia about spiders and snakes."

"That's right," Brian agreed. "Being rich is nothing to be ashamed of, and just because this party isn't going to turn out the way Di planned it, is no reason why everyone shouldn't have a swell time."

"True, true," said Mart. "Personally, I prefer ham and turkey to hamburgers and franks, and as for a couple of dozen waiters hanging around to clean up the mess afterwards, why, that strikes me as a good idea. Isn't there an old saying that nothing is quite so dull as dishwater? Last summer when Brian and I were junior counselors at camp, we must have washed fifty million dishes. Speaking of phobias, I have one very definite phobia about dirty dishes. In fact—"

"Never mind," Trixie interrupted, grinning. "We all know that you cringe at the sight of a kitchen sink and that you spend your nights dreaming up ways to sneak out of the house after meals so that your poor, over-worked sister is stuck with the dirty work."

Mart eyed her critically. "Poor, yes. Overworked, no. But it seems to me, Cinderella, that we have strayed far from the subject of that memorable luncheon you enjoyed out here last spring. Did you bring the subject up simply to stimulate our appetites, or did you have something in mind which you felt was pertinent to the subject of blue-eyed parents?"

111

"You must be a mind reader," Trixie said sarcastically. "In words of one syllable, the answer to your question is yes. After lunch, Di's mother showed me through the house. Di, I remember now, trailed forlornly along behind us, but the point is, when Mrs. Lynch took me through the gallery we spent a lot of time gazing at the portraits of her parents which had been painted by a famous artist whose name I've forgotten."

"What a retentive memory you have, Cinderella!" Mart said, bowing so low that his wig fell off. "Don't tell me you recall whether or not said parents of Mrs. Lynch had blue eyes?"

Trixie shook her head sadly. "My memory isn't that good. But I do remember almost exactly where those portraits were hanging. If the walls weren't draped now, I could lead you boys right to them, and then we'd know for sure."

"Exactly," Mart said. "But since the walls are covered, where does that get us?"

"Don't be such a moron," Trixie cried impatiently. "The musicians in the orchestra will probably have supper when we have ours. This room will be empty then. What's to prevent me from sneaking in here and peering behind that huge bat on the wall over there?"

"Nothing," Mart said, "unless it happens to be your

112

turn to keep Uncle Monty from running things. In which case, I shall be very happy to do the peeking and peering, myself."

"Wait a minute," Jim interrupted. "Peeking isn't going to do any good, unless Trixie happens to know where the master switch is that turns on the lights above the portraits. They're usually in the upper part of each frame, but they're sure to be turned off now. In this dim light you won't be able to tell whether Di's grandparents had blue or black eyes."

"I can use a flashlight," Trixie said promptly.

"Where are you going to get one now, Trixie?" Jim demanded.

"From Di, of course," Trixie said.

"No," Brian said firmly. "Di has got to be left out of this completely until we have definite proof that her uncle is an impostor."

"I forgot about that angle," Trixie admitted. "Well, a candle will do just as well. There are a lot of them in the dining room."

Just then Honey and Mr. Wilson came out of the study across the hall from the gallery. At least Trixie felt pretty sure that they must be Honey and Di's uncle. Honey had donned her devil's mask and black curly wig. Mr. Wilson was wearing a black domino, and was now a small masked cowboy.

At that moment Di appeared with several boys and girls all of whom were masked. They were laughing hilariously because every one of the girls was dressed as a witch and every one of the boys was wearing a cowboy costume.

"Well, podners," Uncle Monty said, joining in the laughter, "great minds think alike, they say. It carries me back to the days of my youth when I was a bronco-buster out west. During one rodeo, a masked cowboy appeared, and, let me tell you, when he roped a steer, it stayed roped. And during the roundup, when the calves are branded, he did the work of ten. That masked cowboy, podners, was yours truly."

Uncle Monty talked on and on while the other guests arrived, and was soon the center of a circle of admiring boys and girls. Even Trixie was momentarily hypnotized by the exciting tales he told. But suddenly Honey whispered in her ear:

"Come into the study with me for a minute, Trixie. It's important."

Holding hands, they slipped out of the circle and into the den. Honey quietly closed the door. Both girls took off their masks and stared at each other. "What on earth is the matter?" Trixie asked.

"That's what's the matter," Honey said. "You keep forgetting to whisper. When you and your brothers

114

and Jim were talking across the hall before the guests arrived, the orchestra was playing loudly, so you didn't have to whisper. But after a while, the orchestra stopped, and you kept right on talking, at the top of your lungs. At least that's the way it sounded to me. I tried to drown out your voices by practically yelling myself, but unless he's stone deaf, which he isn't, Mr. Wilson couldn't help hearing part of what you said. Enough anyway to gather that you're going to look at his parents' portraits in the gallery, and if they both have blue eyes you'll tell Di that he's an impostor."

Trixie sank into the nearest chair. "Oh, no!"

"Oh, *yes*," Honey said, perching on top of the desk. "He pretended he wasn't listening, but I could tell that he was, even after he put on his mask. He was mad, too, Trixie, and I don't blame him. You really ought to stop going around suspecting people all the time. Some day you're going to get into trouble."

"What do you mean, some day?" Trixie demanded. "I'm in trouble right now."

"No, not really," Honey said. "Mr. Wilson was mad because he does lose his temper very easily. But he doesn't stay mad long. He's probably forgotten all about what you said."

"Then you don't think Uncle Monty is an impostor?" Trixie asked.

"Of course not." Honey smiled. "He's very nice when you get to know him. Come on. We'd better get back to the party, Trixie. It sounds as though the grand march were starting."

"I wouldn't miss it for the whole world," Trixie said sarcastically. "I want to be there when Uncle Monty gives himself first prize." She laughed, but inside she was worried. If Mr. Wilson *was* an impostor, what would he do now that he knew she suspected him?

9

A Clue and a Warning

WHEN TRIXIE left Honey, she slipped across the hall and into the dining room. On the long mahogany sideboard was a massive silver candelabrum. Trixie took an orange candle from one of the ornate branches and looked around for some matches. There weren't any in sight. While she was hurriedly searching in the semi-darkened room, Harrison suddenly appeared and turned on the overhead lights. Because both the hall and the dining room were thickly carpeted from wall to wall, Trixie had not heard a sound until the click of the light switch made her jump. As she whirled around, she slipped the candle into her pocket.

Blinking, as her eyes slowly grew accustomed to the brilliant light, she said guiltily, "Oh, hello, Harrison.

118

I didn't expect to find you here."

He gave her a cold, suspicious glance. "Nor did I expect to find *you* here, miss. The other young people are in the gallery where the grand march is in progress," he said so pointedly that Trixie hastily donned her mask and fled back to the gallery.

As she joined the tail end of the grand march, she dismissed the portraits from her mind. The problem now was, for Di's sake, to make sure that the party was a success. Uncle Monty as judge, was standing in the center of the long room. Amid loud laughter he gradually eliminated the boys who had come as famous cowboys. Then he eliminated the girls who had come as witches. The Bob-Whites, in their identical jackets, were eliminated next. That left a girl who had come in a ghost's costume she had made out of an old sheet with a pillowcase for a mask, and a boy who had stitched some rags all over his shirt and jeans. He had started out as quite a convincing-looking beggar, but because he apparently was no handier with a thread and needle than Trixie was, he had shed a few of his rags at every step.

He got the booby prize, and the "ghost," having the most original costume, was awarded the first prize. Uncle Monty tried to make a long speech with the presentation of each prize, but the Bob-Whites drowned out his words by whistling, stamping, and clapping their hands. Trixie guessed that their interruptions annoyed him, but she couldn't be sure because the domino he was wearing hid most of his face.

Then they played the games which he and Honey had planned. Even Trixie had to admit that under Honey's tactful guidance, Uncle Monty made a wonderful master of ceremonies, and the quiz contests were a great success. The orchestra seemed to have as much fun as the guests. Jim won the "sporting songs" group, Brian won the "birds," and Mart quickly got the answers to "famous rivers." In the end every guest won a prize except the three hostesses, Di, Trixie, and Honey, who were not allowed to compete.

Uncle Monty saw to that, and Trixie couldn't help wondering if he had included her as one of his assistants in order to keep an eye on her. He started right off by saying that he wanted the hostesses to remove their masks and wigs. Up until then the Bob-Whites, except for the difference in their heights, had looked exactly alike. And *after* the unmasking, Uncle Monty had hovered close to Trixie's elbow.

Even when all the guests had unmasked and they trooped into the dining room for supper, he stuck to her like a burr. As the boys and girls gathered around the huge table, Harrison switched off the glaring overhead lights. The candle, which Trixie had earlier slipped into the pocket of her jacket, had been replaced. The butler gave her another cold, suspicious glance as he began to light the candles, using a large package of book matches. Trixie stared longingly at the book, hoping he would put it down on the sideboard after he had finished.

But he didn't. Instead he meticulously closed the cover and said to Di, "Will that be all, Miss Diana? Mrs. Lynch said I should have the evening off, but Mr. Wilson thought it best for me to stay until the party had progressed to this point."

"It wasn't necessary for you to stay, Harrison," Di said rather impatiently. "I wish you'd go and take the caterers with you!"

He bowed. "The caterers were not necessary, miss, if I may be so bold as to say so. I am accustomed to handling small affairs like this without assistance." He coughed. "No arrangements had been made for serving refreshments to the members of the orchestra. I have taken the liberty of turning my sitting room over to them. They are now there partaking of a light repast. I hope that is quite satisfactory to you, Miss Lynch."

"Now's my chance," Trixie thought, and started for the door.

As she threaded her way through the crowd,

Uncle Monty somehow arrived at the entrance to the hall ahead of her, blocking her way. He crooked his elbow at her and said with a gallant bow:

"Howdy, podner. It would sure give me pleasure if you would do me the great honor of sitting beside me during supper."

Trixie hesitated. His small, dark-brown eyes were as expressionless as the olive pits they always made her think of, but his thin lips were set in a white line. There was no doubt in her mind now that he knew she suspected him of being an impostor and that he would do everything he could to prevent her from looking at the portraits in the gallery.

As she stood there, trying to make her own face expressionless, he took her hand and led her back to the dining-room table. Trixie shrugged away from him as fast as she could because his hand on hers had felt as cold and scrawny as a chicken's claw. But no matter how hard she tried to mingle with the other boys and girls, she could not evade him. Snakelike, he slithered around after her, attracting attention to her for one reason or another. The first time she tried to leave the room, he scolded her loudly because she hadn't eaten everything on her plate. The second time she rose from her chair he insisted that she must have second helpings of everything. He brought her a plate heaped so high she could hardly hold it on her lap and could hardly be expected to eat it all.

Mart came to her rescue, but while she was transferring a turkey leg and a thick slice of ham to his own plate, Uncle Monty clapped his hands for silence. Two waiters came in from the kitchen then, carrying the dessert on a big silver platter. It was orange sherbet in the form of a giant pumpkin head with chocolate eyes, a cherry nose, and a grinning peppermint stick mouth.

Instead of greeting this surprise with cries of delight, the boys and girls groaned because they had already eaten far too much. Di's face flamed with embarrassment, and Uncle Monty looked as though he were going to hop up and down with rage.

The guests hadn't really meant to be rude; they had simply groaned without thinking. Now, headed by Honey, they crowded around Di and her uncle, praising the dessert and begging for large portions of it. Trixie slipped unobtrusively out of the room.

She knew she couldn't waste time looking for matches, and hoped that the crystal chandeliers in the gallery would shed enough light so she could distinguish the colors in the portraits of Di's grandparents. Slipping and sliding on the polished floor, Trixie raced across the long room to the black drapery which she was sure concealed the portraits. The luminescent bat seemed to be grinning at her evilly as she reached out for the drapery. The moment she gave it a yank, something sprang out at her and she saw to her horror that it was a giant octopus that slapped her in the face before it fell at her feet.

Again Trixie managed to suppress a scream and she gazed thoughtfully down at the hideous papier-mâché creature. Had Uncle Monty purposely planted it behind the drapery?

And then Uncle Monty himself was in the room calling to her as he hurried to her side: "Well, well, podner, what are you doing in here all by your lonesome?" He spoke in a cheerful voice but when he came closer Trixie could see that he was angry.

For answer she picked up the octopus and handed it to him. "Don't you want to fix this so it'll spring out on somebody else?" she asked sweetly. If he put it back behind the drapery she might be able to catch a quick glimpse of the portraits.

"Scared you, huh?" he asked, chuckling, but with the same angry expression in his narrow brown eyes.

Trixie laughed. "Not much. I don't scare easily."

"Oh, you don't, don't you?" he demanded. It was more of a threat than a question, and Trixie would have felt a little frightened if the other guests hadn't come trooping back just then.

She didn't have another chance that evening to look at the portraits, but several times she caught him looking at her with narrowed eyes.

Shortly after midnight Tom Delanoy called for them in the Wheelers' station wagon. "How was the party, kids?" he asked.

"Simply wonderful," Honey told him. "I think everyone at the party had a marvelous time. Don't you think so, too, Trixie?"

Trixie nodded. "I don't usually like parties, but this one was extra special, in spite of Uncle Monty."

"In *spite* of him?" Brian demanded. "Why, he was the life of the party. It wouldn't have been anything without him. He's a grand guy. I like him a lot."

"I do, too," Jim agreed. "I wasn't crazy about those queer things that kept jumping out at people, but once all his silly little traps were sprung, the rest of the evening went very smoothly."

"I suppose you're crazy about him, too, Mart?" Trixie demanded sourly.

"Well, yes and no," Mart replied evasively. "I gather from the piqued expression on your pretty face that you were frustrated in your attempt to ascertain whether or not our hostess's late lamented elderly relatives had orbs the color of yours and mine."

125

Trixie sighed impatiently. "If you mean I didn't get a chance to glance at the portraits, the answer is yes. But one thing is sure. Uncle Monty knows I suspect him, and he was very careful to keep me from looking at the portraits so that proves he's guilty."

Tom groaned and asked Jim, who was sitting on the front seat beside him, "Is she off sleuthing again? If so, I'm going to quit my job."

"Once a sleuth always a sleuth," Jim said and turned around to face Trixie. "Lay off Uncle Monty, Trix. If he's what you think he is, you'll get into trouble, and if he isn't, you'll cause a lot of trouble. *And* unhappiness."

"That's right," Honey agreed. "Di likes him now. She was very proud of him this evening. He was so popular with all of her guests, and so much fun." She shuddered reminiscently. "I didn't like those things that kept jumping out either, Jim. I wish I hadn't screamed when that snake slid across my arm. If he hadn't planted all those horrible things all over the place, the party would have been perfect. I wonder why he did it."

"I can guess," Trixie said. "He wanted the party to be a flop. He'd planned to make us all dance when nobody wanted to. Then he tried to make us play silly kindergarten games, but Honey talked him out of it. If it hadn't been for Honey and the games she

126

suggested, the party would have been a flop."

"I don't get it," Brian said. "It's all too complicated and devious for me."

"It *is* devious," Trixie said. "And Di put her finger on his scheme earlier when she said she hoped her father would give him a lot of money so he'd go away. That's what Uncle Monty hopes, too."

"I don't get it," Brian said again.

"Neither do I," Jim and Honey chorused.

"Oh, don't you see?" Trixie asked impatiently. "He pretends to be very nice to Di, but he's really very mean to her. If he keeps on making her life miserable in that sly way of his, pretty soon Mr. Lynch will give him what he wants so he'll go away."

"What does he want?" Honey asked.

"Money, of course," Trixie said. "What other reason could he have for coming here and posing as Mrs. Lynch's long lost brother?"

"But," Honey objected, "if he isn't Mrs. Lynch's brother, how did he know she ever had one?"

Trixie shrugged. "He could have read about the Lynches in a newspaper or heard about them from a friend who lives in Sleepyside."

Tom parked the station wagon beside the steps leading to the Beldens' terrace. As Trixie and her brothers climbed out, he said, "I gather the Uncle

Monty you kids are talking about is the little guy who arrived up at our place on Saturday morning in a limousine?"

"Yes, Tom," Honey said. "Mr. Montague Wilson. Did you get a chance to talk with him?"

"Not this Saturday, I didn't," Tom said. "But a couple of Saturdays ago, I did."

"But that's not possible, Tom," Honey said. "He only arrived ten days ago. On a Monday night."

"It was on a Saturday, *two weeks* ago," Tom said emphatically.

"What?" Trixie cried, almost shouting.

"Tell us about it," Mart said as he and all the others crowded around the car window.

"It was in the afternoon—at the station," Tom continued. "You see, I was waiting there for Mr. Wheeler who'd gone in to his New York office that morning. I was driving the blue sedan and I guess your friend Mr. Wilson thought it was a taxi." Tom chuckled. "I *was* parked practically in the hack stand space. Anyway, he comes up to me and says, 'Two-ninety-one Hawthorne Street, my good fellow,' with an English accent, and I says, 'Sorry, sir. This is a private car.' He had his hat pulled down over one eye, and that's what made me look at him so closely. Because, unless you're trying to hide your face, you don't wear your hat down

129

over the upper half of it." The young chauffeur laughed. "Take me, for instance, I've got nothing to hide so I wear my cap on the back of my head."

"Hawthorne Street," Brian said. "I never heard of it. Are you sure he gave that address, Tom?"

"I never heard of it either," Tom said. "That's how come I happened to remember it. I thought I knew every street in this town, so being as curious as Trixie, I made a mental note of the address and decided I would look it up some day."

"Did you?" Trixie asked.

"No," he said, "and don't you go looking it up either, Trixie Belden."

"Why not?" Trixie demanded.

"Because," he said, "I asked a friend of mine who's a cop, about it. Webster. You Belden kids must know him. Webster's the cop who used to be on duty in front of the grade school."

They all nodded. "Spider" Webster was one of the most popular policemen in town.

"He's on night duty now," Tom continued. "On the outskirts of town where Main Street merges with the main highway. Anyway, he says Hawthorne Street is the worst street in town. Most people call it Skid Row. Nothing but ramshackle houses where bums live when they're not in jail. And two-ninety-one has the worst reputation of them all. It's a crummy hotel run by a shady character named Olyfant." Tom leaned out of the car window to shake his finger at Trixie warningly. "Sleuth around in your imagination all you like, Trixie Belden. But if you know what's good for you, steer clear of Hawthorne Street!"

10

Bad News

IT DOESN'T mean a thing," Honey said firmly. "And you know perfectly well the boys agree with me. Tom was mistaken, that's all."

It was a warm, sunny morning and right after a late breakfast, the girls had met at the clubhouse so that Honey could measure the windows for the curtains she planned to make.

"I don't care what the boys think," Trixie said. "They're not *always* right. I'm as sure as sure can be that Tom was not mistaken." She placed the stepladder beside one of the windows and, with one hand on each side of the ladder, steadied it as Honey climbed up.

"But Tom admitted himself," Honey said, "that the man he saw at the station two weeks ago wore his hat

132

pulled down so that his face was half hidden. Tom also reported that he spoke with an English accent, which Uncle Monty definitely doesn't.''

"He doesn't really speak with a western accent either," Trixie said. "Did you notice how he pronounced rodeo? Well, out West, Honey, it's always pronounced ro-*day*-o; never *ro*deo.''

"Both ways are right," Honey argued.

Trixie ignored her. "And all that podner stuff. It's phony. Everything he knows about ranches he got out of books.''

"That's where you got your own information," Honey pointed out. "So how can you consider yourself a good judge?''

"I don't pretend to be," Trixie replied. "But when Regan says a man has never been on a horse, you can be sure that said man never was.''

Honey perched on top of the stepladder and frowned down at Trixie. "All right," she said. "Maybe Uncle Monty wasn't a broncobuster. I'll admit he exaggerates, and some of the stories he told last night were fantastic. But that still doesn't make him an impostor.''

"No," Trixie admitted. "But the fact that he came to town ahead of time does.''

Honey gasped. "If you say one word to Di about that awful hotel on Hawthorne Street, Trixie Belden,

I—I'll just never forgive you."

Trixie grinned. "What *can* I say about it? I've never been there myself." She added in a lower voice, "The first chance I get I *am* going there."

Honey looked horrified. "Oh, no, Trixie, you wouldn't dare!"

"I've got to," Trixie answered calmly. "Right now we can't prove that Uncle Monty ever went near Skid Row. But I'm positive that he did stay there until he suddenly arrived at the Lynches' the following Monday evening."

"That doesn't make sense," Honey objected. "Why didn't he go straight from the train station to his sister's home?"

Trixie shrugged. "Do you know what 'casing the joint' means, Honey?"

"No, I don't," Honey said rather crossly.

"You should read more detective stories," Trixie said. "When crooks plan to rob a home, they first case it. In other words, they find out what the family's habits are, the best time to commit the robbery, how to get in and out most easily, and so forth. I'm just as sure as sure can be that Uncle Monty came to town ahead of time so he could first contact his friends on Hawthorne Street and find out all he could about the Lynch family."

Honey looked impressed. "Then you think he plans to rob them?"

"Not if he can get a lot of money from Mr. Lynch," Trixie replied. "If Mr. Lynch won't give him any, I'll bet he steals as much as he can and then disappears." She leaned forward and added in a whisper, "Did you ever wonder why Uncle Monty came out to your place last Saturday, Honey?"

"He came out to look at the horses, of course," Honey said.

Trixie grinned. "That was his excuse. I think he came out here to case your joint."

Honey climbed down the ladder, nervously winding the tape measure around her slim wrist. "I think you're crazy, Trixie. Why should he want to rob us when he can steal from the Lynches so easily?"

"I don't think he himself plans to break into your house," Trixie said, "but he could pass along any information he picks up to a pal of his. Someone who lives in that hotel on Hawthorne Street. Olyfant, for instance. The man Tom said was a shady character."

Honey covered her face with both hands. "Please, Trixie, stop using that underworld language. It always gives me the jitters."

Trixie laughed. "There's nothing for you to be jittery about. It didn't take Uncle Monty long to realize that

135

this is not a good place to try and rob. He couldn't help noticing that besides your father and Jim, two men sleep on the place. Regan and Tom. Also, he saw Jim's dog, Patch. Also that you have a lot of servants. Robbing this place would be about as simple as attempting to break into the White House."

Honey sighed with relief. "The Lynches have the same sort of place, only more so."

"Yes," Trixie said, "but Uncle Monty doesn't have to break into it. He's there. And didn't you notice, Honey, that the Lynches have a lot of valuable things lying around? Your home is beautiful but it isn't all cluttered up with little knickknacks. I don't mean just the silver on their sideboard. I'm talking about those antique bronze and porcelain things that are all over the place. Why, Di told me herself that those china birds in Mr. Lynch's study are so rare that a museum offered her mother thousands of dollars for the collection."

Honey nodded. "I know that the dessert service is worth a small fortune. I have seen some of those royal blue and gold plates that are decorated with tropical birds in museums. And I've seen some of those gold-trimmed goblets in museums."

"Don't forget the paintings in the gallery," Trixie added. "Some of them are museum pieces, too. What's to prevent Uncle Monty from cutting them from their frames some night and walking out with them?"

Honey smiled. "That room is always locked except on special occasions so he couldn't take those. Di told me so last night."

"Oh," Trixie cried in a disappointed tone of voice. "That ruins everything."

"What do you mean?" Honey demanded.

"Now I can't get a look at her grandparents' portraits." Trixie frowned. "I thought Di would probably invite us out to lunch or something pretty soon, and I'd get a chance to sneak into the gallery."

"Well, if she does," Honey said cheerfully, "all I have to do is ask her to show me the paintings. She must know where the key is kept. And if she doesn't, she can get it from her mother."

"How smart you are," Trixie said. "I've already been through the gallery, but you haven't." She grabbed Honey's arm. "Let's call up Di now and hint around for an invite. I can't wait to find out if her grandparents both had blue eyes."

Honey giggled. "I can't wait to find out that you're wrong about that. But where are your manners, Miss Belden? Nice young ladies don't hint for invitations."

Trixie sniffed. "I'm not a lady. You don't need me to help you measure these windows. I'm only keeping

137

you from your job. So if it's okay, I'll go up to the house now and give Di a ring." She raced off before Honey had a chance to object.

Tom Delanoy was raking the leaves on the front lawn and hailed Trixie as she ran toward the house. "Where's the fire, Trix?"

Trixie stopped to catch her breath. "No fire, Tom. Unless you're talking about that old saying that where there's smoke there must be fire."

He leaned on his rake, grinning. "I suppose by that remark, you're trying to lead the topic of conversation back to where we dropped it after the Halloween party last night?"

Trixie nodded. "Uncle Monty."

"In that case," Tom said, "the old saying that applies best is 'Birds of a feather flock together.' "

Trixie nodded again, vigorously. "You're sure he was the man you spoke to at the station two weeks ago, aren't you?"

Tom thought for a minute. "No, I'm not sure, Trix. And I'm sorry I said what I did last night. If you kids are going to blab it all over the village, I'll end up with a nice libel suit on my neck."

"We won't repeat a word of what you said," Trixie said hastily. "On account of Di, you know. She's very sensitive, especially about Uncle Monty."

Tom mopped his brow, obviously relieved. "Thank goodness for that! If Mr. Wheeler ever knew what a fool I was last night, he'd fire me. I know he would. And I like this job, Trix."

"I know you do," Trixie said sympathetically. "The Wheelers are wonderful people. And you must know, Tom, that Honey and Jim and we Beldens would never do anything to get you into trouble."

"I know," he said, "especially since it was you kids who got me the job. The thing is, Trix, I said what I did for your sake. You're quite a little detective. There's no sense in denying it. I felt that sooner or later you'd find out that Uncle Monty has—I mean someone who looks an awful lot like him—has friends on Hawthorne Street. It's not too safe even in the day-time for a kid like you. If you feel you have to snoop around, get one of your brothers to go with you. Or better yet, let them go by themselves. That's why I said what I did in front of them."

Trixie's mouth fell open with surprise. "Are you implying, Tom, that Uncle Monty has gone back to Hawthorne Street since he's been living out at the Lynches'?"

"I'm not implying anything at all, Trixie," Tom said firmly.

"Then how else," Trixie asked, "could I possibly

140

have found out that he—or someone who looks like him—has friends there? I mean, unless you told me?"

Tom squinted up at the sun in the bright blue sky. "You've been known to trail people, haven't you? Well, all I'm saying is, don't trail this suspect." Abruptly he changed the subject. "Now, Trixie, about that cottage down by the road."

Trixie blinked. "What about it, Tom?"

Still avoiding her eyes, he said, "You kids spend a lot of time in it, and so far as I can see, you've spent a lot of money fixing it up."

Trixie started to say something but he held up one hand to silence her. "I don't want to pry into your secrets, but, well, you know that Celia and I plan to get married some day, and well, the truth of the matter is, Mr. Wheeler said we could have the old gatehouse."

"Oh, no," Trixie moaned.

Tom looked almost as unhappy as she did. "I'm sorry about this, Trixie, but what can I do? Celia is crazy about the place."

"Since we fixed it up," Trixie said bitterly. "It was nothing but a tumbledown shack before."

"I can't help that," Tom said miserably. "She was down there early this morning measuring the windows for curtains."

Trixie collapsed on a mound of autumn leaves.

"That's what Honey is doing right now. Oh, Tom, it's our secret clubhouse!"

Tom laughed without humor. "It didn't take a very detective mind to figure that out. And Honey's not the type to whine to her old man saying that you kids want to keep it."

"She'd die first," Trixie said staunchly.

Tom took a deep breath. "I'll pay you back every cent you spent, and for your time, too. You could build yourselves another clubhouse somewhere else where it would be more secret, couldn't you?"

Trixie got up and dusted off the seat of her jeans. "I don't know, Tom," she said hopelessly. "I'll talk it over with the boys and let you know."

Shoulders drooping, she slouched discouragedly into the house and called the Lynches' phone number. Harrison answered:

"Who's calling, please?"

"Trixie Belden."

"I'll see if Miss Diana is in," he said.

Trixie, slumped over the telephone table in the study, waited. It was an awful blow to lose the clubhouse when they had worked so hard on it and had slaved to earn the money for the necessary repairs. It was all very well for Tom to say that they could build another one somewhere else, but soon it would be winter with snow and sleet and ice and between now and then only weekends and a few hours of daylight after school.

"Miss Belden?" The butler's voice was as cold as the ice Trixie had been thinking about. "Miss Diana is not in—*to you!*"

Stunned, Trixie heard the click as he hung up.

11

Hawthorne Street

TRIXIE SAT in the Wheelers' study, too stunned to move. She was still clutching the telephone when Jim came in a few moments later.

"What's the matter with you?" he asked, grinning. "How come you're literally and figuratively glued to the phone on a nice day like this?"

Trixie hastily placed the instrument back in its cradle. The sight of Jim brought back the depressing news about the clubhouse, crowding all other thoughts from her mind.

"Oh, Jim," she cried. "Have you heard? Mr. Wheeler has given the cottage—our secret clubhouse—to Tom and Celia!"

Jim clutched his red hair with both hands. "Since

144

when? And are you sure of that?"

Trixie nodded sadly. "Tom just told me a few minutes ago. It's not really his fault. Celia is crazy about the place. I don't know how she happened to see our clubhouse, Jim, but—"

"I do," Jim said. "Bobby! Last Sunday he spent a lot of time in the kitchen consuming cookies and milk. It was while you girls were making plans for the Halloween party. I happened to pass through the kitchen once and I heard him tell Celia that he had been very busy 'holping' us 'jingle' the roof of our 'see-crud' clubhouse."

Trixie sighed with exasperation. "Brian and Mart should have had better sense than to take Bobby with them when they moved all that stuff from our garage last Saturday."

Jim chuckled. "It's a known fact in this neck of the woods that Bobby and a secret are soon parted. But that's the price you have to pay for having a lovable kid brother like Bobby. And there's no sense in crying over spilled milk, Trix."

"I do feel like crying," Trixie stormed. "Not because of Bobby. I'm used to getting into scrapes on account of him. But it's not fair. Celia wouldn't have looked at the gatehouse twice if we hadn't fixed it up. Before it was just a shack."

Jim shrugged. "All's fair in love and war, I guess. Actually, before we spent so much time and money on it, we should have figured we'd have to ask Dad if we could keep it."

Trixie sniffed. "Why must you always be so honorable all of the time, Jim? It gets boring. If you'd asked Mr. Wheeler for permission to keep the cottage it wouldn't have been a secret. Not that it is. Why, even Dad knows about it. And I suppose it was Bobby who told him, too. Di doesn't know how lucky she is to have two nurses on her place who spend all their time keeping her kid brothers out of her hair."

Jim stared up at the ceiling. "You don't really mean that, Trix. Now calm down and start trying to make some sense."

"Oh, all right," Trixie cried. "But I'll never forgive Celia, even if Tom did say he would pay us for our time and money."

"Well, that's a break," Jim said cheerfully. "I don't blame you for being mad, Trixie. You put twenty-five dollars of your own money in our clubhouse. Money you worked hard all last summer to earn. The rest of us haven't contributed nearly as much. I'm glad you're going to get your share back."

"Don't be ridic," Trixie said. "It's not the money I'm worried about. What bothers me is what we are going to do between now and next spring, which is about as soon as you boys will be able to start working on another clubhouse."

Jim sighed. "Frankly, I don't know, Trix. And in the meantime, what are you Beldens going to do with all of the sports equipment Brian and Mart brought down from your garage last weekend? I don't know where you could store them."

"We'll just have to donate it to the scrap drive," Trixie said forlornly.

"That can't happen," Jim said firmly. "Skis, sleds, ice skates, snowshoes, a pup tent, outdoor cooking utensils—" He spread his hands. "Those things look old and tired now, but it will run into a lot of money when you try to replace them with new ones."

"You're telling me," Trixie said sarcastically. "But, Jim, there isn't room at our place for them. And if we leave them outdoors they'll be ruined."

Jim took her hand and led her out through the French doors to the veranda. "There isn't room up here for them either, Trix. You couldn't safely put another thing in the cellar, attic, stable, garage, tool-house, or even the boathouse. I know because Dad and I have been inspecting the premises on account of Fire Prevention Week." He pulled her down beside him on the swing. "But relax, kid. As Micawber would

say, 'Something is bound to turn up.' "

Trixie groaned. "I wish you and Honey had never decided to read *David Copperfield* together. All you seem to do is quote from it. All *I* can remember about Micawber is that he spent most of his time in debtors' prison. A cheerful thought!"

"That's not all you remember about *David Copperfield,*" Jim said, laughing. "Last night you said Uncle Monty reminded you of the villain Uriah Heep. Do you still think that Di's uncle is as slippery as an eel, Trix? I mean, do you still think that he's an impostor?"

"Yes, I do," Trixie said. "And I'll prove it some day. Wait and see."

Jim narrowed his green eyes. "As Tom said last night, sleuth around in your imagination all you like, but steer clear of Hawthorne Street. You'll have to promise me that, Trixie."

Trixie hastily changed the subject. "We'd better call a meeting of the B.W.G.'s right away, Jim, and decide what to do about a clubhouse."

"That," he agreed, "is the most important thing on the agenda right now. We'd better call a meeting at once. Where is everybody?"

"Honey," Trixie told him, "is down at the clubhouse measuring the windows for the curtains. I can't bear to tell her the bad news. She bought the material ages ago with the money she earned working as her mother's secretary. You remember all those letters Honey answered, don't you, Jim? She worked two whole weekends so she could buy that stuff that looks sort of like gunny-sacking to me. What's it called?"

"Monk's cloth," Jim said. "It's expensive, but it's just exactly what we want, Trixie. It's a neutral shade and it wears forever."

"Oh, I think it's swell material," Trixie said. "I'd have died if Honey had wanted to hang gingham or dainty ruffled curtains. It just isn't that kind of a clubhouse. But," she added miserably, "Celia will probably have all sorts of frilly ideas. Organdy and such. Ugh!"

"Celia has very good taste," Jim said sternly. "But that's not the point. We've got to have a meeting right away. Where are Brian and Mart?"

"They ought to be here soon," Trixie said as they started down the veranda steps. "When last seen they were cleaning the chicken coop. At least Brian was. Mart was sitting on an upturned pail giving him directions."

Jim laughed. "That situation didn't last long, I'll bet. Knowing Brian, Mart did his share of the work, so they ought to be through by now."

"You're so right," Trixie said, pointing toward the stable. "Here they come, and Mart does look as though

150

he'd moved an arm muscle or two."

"Hi," Mart greeted Trixie and Jim. "Why are you two so glum? One would think Brian had been slave-driving you instead of poor me."

"Glum is the word," Trixie replied. "We've lost the clubhouse!"

Brian stared at her as though she had lost her mind. "What are you talking about? Houses don't go around getting lost."

Mart gazed up at the sky. "Haven't seen any cyclones around recently. Or tornadoes. And the gentle little breeze that wafted into my window this morning wasn't exactly a hurricane." He shrugged, waving his hands. "But of course, Trix, if you say the clubhouse is gone, why it's gone. Poof! Vanished into thin air."

"Oh, cut it out," Brian commanded and appealed to Jim. "What's Trixie trying to tell us?"

Jim explained, but no sooner had he finished than Honey appeared and had to be told the bad news all over again. Then they all began talking at once.

"It's just not possible," Honey wailed, sinking down on the grassy lawn. "I always thought Celia was one of our best friends."

"And the gatehouse was such a perfect place," Mart said. "Who would have thought that anybody else would have it as a gift?"

"It was perfect," Brian agreed, "but let's think of it in the past tense from now on definitely. It isn't ours. It never was, really, so that's that."

Trixie tossed her sandy curls. "I don't think we should give up so easily. Let's go down there and make it so hideous Celia will never want to go near it again. I feel like gouging holes in the floors."

"That's a good idea," Mart said sarcastically. "Especially since the floors are dirt. Even Bobby would be able to replace your divots without too much trouble."

"Then let's smear tar all over the walls," Trixie suggested, half-laughing, half-serious. "Gallons and gallons of nice sticky, smelly, black tar ought to do the trick!"

Honey frowned up at her. "I don't see how you can joke, Trixie, when everything is so perfectly awful. "

"That's right," Jim said. "Let's try to make some sense for a change."

But although they spent most of the weekend trying to figure out how to solve this new problem, they got nowhere. Honey kept saying, "There's plenty of land." And Jim would reply, "But the ground will be frozen soon." Then Brian would say, "We *could* knock together a shack, but we don't want that."

Mart finally summed it up: "Let's let it simmer in our subconscious minds until next Saturday and hold an-

152

other meeting then. We're all too stunned right now to make sense."

Trixie was only too glad to second this motion. She herself hadn't been able to contribute anything in the way of ideas at the meeting because her thoughts were so jumbled. Somehow she had to prove that Uncle Monty was an impostor, but first of all she wanted to find out why Di refused to come to the phone on Saturday.

It didn't make sense, unless Harrison, because he didn't approve of her, had deliberately lied. "Harrison never did like me," Trixie reflected. "And now, since he knows that I swiped a candle from the dining room at the party, he probably has decided that I'm not exactly fit company for Di."

For once in her life, Trixie was glad to go to school on Monday morning. Di was not on the bus, but there was nothing unusual about that. As often as not, she traveled to and from school in the limousine.

When the bus stopped in front of the school, Trixie was the first one off. She tore into the locker room, and, as she had hoped, found Di there. Suddenly Trixie was tongue-tied. All weekend she had planned just what she would say at this very moment, but now all she could get out was: "Oh, hello, Di."

Diana carefully placed her coat on a hanger inside

153

her locker and slammed the door. "Don't you speak to me, Trixie Belden," she said and swept past her without another word.

Trixie's heart sank. Harrison hadn't lied after all. Honey came into the locker room then and Trixie said, "Di isn't speaking to me. I didn't say anything about it before, Honey, but when I called her from your house on Saturday she wouldn't come to the phone. And I don't know why, Honey."

Honey gasped. "Oh, Trixie, you've hurt her feelings. She knows you think her uncle is an impostor and a thief and everything."

Trixie shook her head. "She can't know unless one of us told her, and none of us would since we know how she feels about Uncle Monty."

The bell rang then, and they hurried off to their homeroom. All morning Trixie wandered from class to class in a daze. During classes she never once raised her hand, and when called on for answers, she stumbled and stuttered and was sternly frowned upon. The math instructor did more than frown. She said crossly: "Trixie, I'm sorry but you can't go home on the bus today. You'll have to see me after school. Please call your mother during lunch and arrange for some other transportation."

Meekly, Trixie said, "Yes, Miss Golden," but she

wasn't really listening. So she completely forgot to call her mother during the lunch hour. It was Honey who reminded her that Miss Golden wanted to see her just as she was about to board the bus.

"Gleeps," Trixie yelled and grabbed Mart's arm as he tried to push past her. "Tell Moms I've got to stay after school. I'll come home C.O.D. in a cab if there's anything left of me."

As it turned out Miss Golden was not cross; she was simply disappointed. "You've got an excellent mind, Trixie," she said, "when you concentrate. Are you worried about something?"

"Yes," Trixie said truthfully. "One of my best friends is mad at me."

Miss Golden laughed. "Well, kiss and make up, and see if you can't concentrate a little more in class tomorrow, dear."

"I will," Trixie promised and hurried down to the locker room. Suddenly it all dawned on her. Uncle Monty was the answer, of course. It was he who had turned Di against her. And the reason was obvious. He didn't want Trixie to be invited out to the Lynches' house again. He didn't want her to have any opportunity of looking at those portraits in the gallery. He wasn't taking any chances at all. With Di not speaking to her, Trixie couldn't even ask her any questions which might be embarrassing to Uncle Monty. He felt he was safe when Trixie was not around.

If he was an impostor.

Trixie was surer than ever now that he was. She slipped on her jacket and left the school without telephoning for a cab. If she didn't arrive home for an hour or more, no one would worry. If she couldn't get the proof she wanted in one way, she would get it in another.

On Sunday Trixie had carefully inspected the maps in the glove compartment of her father's car, so she knew exactly where Hawthorne Street was. Almost running, she set off for that part of town. But when she left Main Street and turned into the alley that led to it, she slowed to a walk. It was a narrow, winding alley, with sidewalks that were lined on both sides by two-story houses that were so rickety they made Trixie feel as though they might topple down on her head any minute.

"There's nothing to be afraid of," Trixie said to herself firmly. "This used to be a cowpath once. I'm going to pretend that all these strange-looking people are harmless cows."

The people who were sitting on the stoops and the sagging porches *were* strange-looking, but they stared at Trixie as though she were the one who was odd. The

women, in their bright shawls and full skirts, looked like gypsies, and the men, when they moved at all, shuffled as though their feet hurt. Even the children moved slowly and stared suspiciously at Trixie as she passed by.

She began to walk faster after a while and at the same time she wished she had gone straight home from school. Suddenly the narrow alley ended and before her lay a long straight street. A dusty sign told her that it was Hawthorne Street.

Trixie glanced at the houses and suppressed a shudder. They were no worse than the dilapidated buildings in the alley, but there was something evil about them. The accumulated dirt of years clung to them, and there wasn't a single solitary soul in sight. But Trixie sensed that people were watching her from behind those filthy, curtainless windows. She forced herself to keep moving and realized that she was shuffling along the street just as the men in the alley behind her had shuffled.

"It's the air around here," she thought. "It's absolutely stifling. It makes me feel as though it's not even worthwhile breathing."

There were no porches or stoops here. Although the tarnished brass numerals on the doors were clogged with dirt, they were so close that they were easy to read. The first one Trixie glanced at was two-o-one, and then almost before she realized it, she had stopped in front of two-ninety-one. At that same moment the door was opened and a man came out.

Because the door opened right onto the narrow sidewalk, and Trixie had stopped right in front of it, he almost stepped on her toes. She drew back just in time and said, "I'm sorry."

Inwardly she thought, "I'm a lot more sorry than you think. I wish I'd taken Tom's advice and stayed away from here." Her knees were shaking because the man was so ugly and the street was so silent. He was wearing a tight-fitting shiny blue suit and had obviously not shaved for several days. His eyebrows were so bushy and black they seemed to merge with his eyelashes, giving Trixie the impression that he was wearing a black domino. Trixie shuddered as he stared at her.

And then she realized that he was as startled by the sight of her as she had been by the sight of him. Instantly her legs stopped shaking, and although she had no idea who this strange and ugly man was, she said, "I guess you must be Mr. Olyfant."

He glared at her through his mask of eyebrows and eyelashes. "What's it to you if I am?"

Too late Trixie realized that she had no answer to

159

this question. She had come to this sordid place without making plans, hoping that somehow she could get some proof that Uncle Monty was an impostor. There were probably lots of clues inside the hotel, but she knew now that she would never have the courage to enter the door even if she were invited to do so. Weakly she said, "I was just wondering. That's all."

Carefully he took a cigarette from his pocket and lighted it. "Anything else you want to know?" His voice was both insolent and nonchalant, but Trixie noticed that his hands were trembling.

Shrewdly she guessed that he wished she would go away just as much as she wished she had never come. As she stared at his hands she realized with a start that the book matches he was holding were exactly like those which Harrison had used when he lighted the candles in the dining room at Di's party. The flap was royal blue with "The Lynches" printed on it in big, sprawling gold letters.

Trixie knew that she could not possibly be mistaken. For several minutes on Halloween she had gazed longingly at the matches when Harrison closed the flap, hoping that he would put them down somewhere within reach so she could borrow them. She remembered thinking that the matches must have been very expensive. They were outsize to begin with, and the gold lettering was very distinctive.

How had a package of those personalized matches got into the pocket of this ugly man coming out of this dingy building on Hawthorne Street?

12

A Narrow Escape

TRIXIE QUICKLY decided that there could be only one answer to the question. As Tom Delanoy had hinted, Uncle Monty had come back to Hawthorne Street after he arrived at the Lynches'. During one of his visits, without realizing it, he must have left behind in the hotel a package of those personalized matches.

As though reading her mind, the ugly man glanced sharply at the flap and hastily tucked the book into his pocket. Then his hand shot out and closed around Trixie's wrist.

"Listen, girlie," he said in a menacing tone of voice, "I guess you and I had better go inside my hotel and have a little talk."

Trixie was terrified, but she made up her mind that

she wouldn't let him know it. "So you *are* Mr. Olyfant?"

He nodded. "And who are you?"

"Trixie Belden," she told him coolly although she was sure he could hear the wild beating of her heart. "My father works in the bank."

Olyfant's bushy eyebrows shot up. "Peter Belden's kid, huh? I've read about you in the newspaper. Fancy yourself as quite a little detective, don't you?" The eyebrows came down again. "I'd say you were a snoop, and I don't like snoops. Are you coming inside with me, now, or do I have to drag you?"

"My mother," Trixie continued just as though he hadn't interrupted, "expected me home from school an hour ago. She's probably so worried about me she must have already called the police. You'd better let me go!"

A disagreeable smile twitched his lips. "So nobody knows where you are?" His grip on her wrist tightened and he pulled her a step toward the hotel.

Trixie's pounding heart missed a beat. *Nobody did.* She forced her own lips into an impudent smile. "Don't worry," she said, "it won't take the police long to track me to your horrible hotel. A lot of people saw me turn off Main Street into that alley back there, and practically everybody in the alley stared at me as I walked down into this street. If you don't let me go, this place will be swarming with cops in a few minutes."

He snatched his hand away from her. "Scram," he hissed. "Get out of here as fast as you can and don't ever come back."

Trixie was only too glad to obey his orders. But although she wanted to turn and run as fast as she could, she forced herself to move slowly. She could feel his eyes boring into her back until she mingled with the people in the crowded alley. Now they didn't seem strange at all; they seemed like the most friendly and the most pleasant people in the world.

"After that awful Olyfant," Trixie reflected with a grin, "even a tribe of cannibals would look nice to me."

A cab was parked on the corner of Main Street and she gratefully climbed inside. Weak with relief because at last she was really safe, she sank back against the cushions and stared at her shaking hands. Gradually they stopped shaking as Trixie's spirits rose. Getting the proof she needed had been worth the terrifying few minutes she had spent in front of Olyfant's hotel. There was no doubt in her mind now that it was Uncle Monty whom Tom had seen at the station that afternoon.

The cab stopped at the Beldens' back terrace, and Mart, looking very cross, came down the terrace steps and paid the taxi driver.

"Listen, lamebrain," he began and then, as she sank

down on the low stone wall of the terrace, "Gleeps! You look as though you'd seen a ton of ghosts. What happened? Are you going to flunk math this term?"

Trixie opened her mouth to tell him about her frightening experience, and then changed her mind. Mart could be very sympathetic at times, but she sensed that this wasn't one of those times. "Is Moms mad at me because I had to stay after school to talk to Miss Golden?" Trixie asked in a quavering voice.

"She doesn't even know it," Mart said disgustedly. "How could you have forgotten, you dope? She and her prize mums are at the Garden Club show. Which means that you owe me a buck. Seventy-five cents for the taxi, and a quarter for taking care of Bobby."

"Oh, oh," Trixie thought, *"how could I have forgotten the flower show? Suppose Brian and Mart hadn't come straight home from school? Bobby would have been all alone this whole past hour!"* She shuddered. Bobby, when left to his own resources for even a short time, usually managed to get himself into some sort of scrape. Very often these scrapes amounted to narrow escapes.

"I'm sorry, Mart," Trixie said contritely. "I'll pay you back as soon as I get my allowance on Saturday. And thanks for taking over for me."

"I've a good mind to charge you double for baby-sitting," Mart said. "Or should I say fiend-sitting? Wait till you hear—"

The phone rang then and Trixie hurried inside to answer it.

It was Honey. "Can you come up right away? I have something very important to tell you."

"I can't," Trixie said. "I was supposed to come straight home from school to take care of Bobby while Moms is at the Garden Club show. I forgot, and Mart has been stuck with him, and he's furious. Can't you come down here to tell me, Honey?"

"In a sec," Honey said, and hung up.

Trixie hurried up to her room and changed her skirt for jeans. Bobby was playing in his room across the hall and he yelled at her:

"Hey! Where you been?"

"Oh, around," Trixie said vaguely. "Did Mart give you your orange juice to drink?"

Bobby came into her room dragging a very worn giant panda behind him. "Nope. Mart didn't gived it to me. I gived it to my own self."

"How smart of you!" Trixie gave him a hug. "You're getting very grown up since you started school."

"I squoozed it my own self, too," he said, proudly holding out his hands. On every finger was a bandage. "I cutted myself with that great big kitchen knife but

166

I didn't cry at all. I didn't yell either."

Mart appeared then. "In the two minutes that elapsed between the arrival of his bus and our bus, he managed to create a shambles. I don't know how he does it."

"Bobby," Trixie cried, holding him close to her. "You know you're not supposed to touch knives." Guiltily she thought, "If he'd cut himself badly it would have been all my fault. I've got to stop going around in a daze or something awful will happen."

Honey called to her from the terrace, and Trixie yelled out the window, "Come up to my room." She guided Bobby back across the hall. "Play with your toys like a good boy for just a little while, then I'll give you a long ride on my bike."

Mart greeted Honey at the top of the stairs. "You girls are certainly acting suspiciously. First Trix arrives from the village looking as though she'd seen a ghost. Then Honey arrives gasping for breath. What gives, girls?"

He waited a minute and when neither of them replied, galloped downstairs.

Once the girls were alone in Trixie's room, Honey exploded. "Oh, Trixie, you were absolutely right about Di's uncle. He's a terrible man. I called her up after I got home from school to find out why she's mad at you, and do you know what?"

Trixie carefully closed the door and sank down on her bed. "No, but I can guess."

"He told her a lot of lies about you," Honey continued in an outraged voice. "After the party Friday night he said that you said a lot of mean things about her and her mother. He said you made fun of their house and their clothes and just about everything!"

Trixie sighed. "I hope you told her that I didn't do anything of the kind."

"I tried to," Honey said forlornly, "but she wouldn't listen. I couldn't very well come out and say that her mother's brother is a liar." She clenched her slim hands. "If only we had some proof."

"We have," Trixie said. "At least I think it's proof." She told Honey about her dangerous adventure on Hawthorne Street that afternoon.

Honey's hazel eyes were wide. "You're right, Trixie. How else could those matches have got into that horrid Olyfant man's pocket?" She lowered her voice. "I take it you didn't tell Mart?"

Trixie shook her head. "He'd say there were a lot of people named Lynch in town. Or he could say that one of the servants left the matches in the dogwagon and somebody from Hawthorne Street picked them up, or something like that—just a simple explanation. You know how awfully logical the boys always are."

Honey nodded. "Anyway, I'm on your side now, Trixie. I'm sure Uncle Monty is an impostor. I think we ought to go straight to Mr. Lynch and tell him everything we know about this man."

"We can't do that," Trixie said, "because we still haven't got any real proof. Not any concrete evidence. He'd probably laugh at that match clue. Worse still, he'd tell Dad that I'd been snooping around Skid Row." Trixie shuddered. "Boy, would I get the dickens!"

"There's only one thing to do," Honey said thoughtfully. "Di invited me to spend Wednesday night with her. I'll ask her mother to show me through the gallery. And if the portraits of her parents show that they had blue eyes, I'll go straight to Mr. Lynch."

"Okay," Trixie said sadly. "How I envy you! I wish I could be in at the kill."

"It's a shame," Honey said sympathetically. "But maybe there won't be any kill. Maybe one of the parents had brown eyes. Then what?"

"Let's worry about that when it happens," Trixie said. "Personally I can't wait until you find out for sure on Wednesday night."

"Neither can I," Honey agreed. "There are phones all over that house. If we get the proof we need, I'll call you up right after I talk to Mr. Lynch."

"I don't think I can live till then," Trixie said. "It's going to be awfully hard to try and behave as though nothing exciting was going to happen on Wednesday night. That's more than forty-eight hours away. I can't bear the suspense."

Bobby burst into her room then without knocking. "Hey," he greeted them. "When you gonna give me that bike ride, Trixie?"

Trixie glared at him. "Bobby Belden! You go right back out into the hall, close my door, and knock. Honestly, you're getting so spoiled you'll grow up without any manners at all!"

He glared back at her. "Won't! I tried to knock but it hurted and it didn't make any noise." He held out his bandaged hands for Honey to see.

Honey gasped. "Oh, good heavens, Bobby! You haven't got cuts on every single finger, have you?"

"Sure," he said proudly. "Thumbs, too."

Remembering what a narrow escape he had had earlier that afternoon with the big, sharp kitchen knife, Trixie flushed with shame. "All right, Bobby," she said. "You go bring my bike down from the garage. Then I'll give you a ride."

"Okey dokey," he said and darted off.

Trixie sighed. "Life must go on, I suppose. I'll probably be doing something mundane like homework when you call me from the Lynches' with the exciting news that both of Di's grandparents had blue eyes."

But although Trixie stayed awake until eleven o'clock Wednesday night, the phone did not ring. When she arrived at school Thursday morning, Di and Honey were waiting for her in the locker room.

Di promptly threw her arms around Trixie. "Oh, I'm so sorry I was mad at you," she cried contritely. "Please forgive me, Trix!"

"Sure," Trixie replied, embarrassed and pleased at the same time. "But what happened?"

"We can't talk about it here," Di whispered. "Can you come home with me after school, Trixie, and spend the night?"

"I'd love to," Trixie said enthusiastically. "I'll call Moms during lunch and see if it's all right."

The bell rang then and the girls didn't get another chance to talk until noon. Trixie raced to the nearest phone booth, and a few minutes later emerged, grinning. "Moms says it's all right as long as we don't talk all night." She tucked her hands through Di's and Honey's arms. "I'm too excited to eat. Tell me all about everything that happened last night."

"It's too long a story," Di said, "and there're too many people around." She squeezed Trixie's hand. "The important thing right now is that you're not mad

171

at me. I was so afraid you would be."

"Why should I be?" Trixie demanded.

"Because," Di said, flushing, "I was silly enough to believe you'd said mean things about me and my mother." She lowered her voice. "I hate Uncle Monty. I *hate* him! And I know now that he *is* an impostor."

13

Blue Eyes — or Brown!

DI REFUSED to say another word about her uncle until later that afternoon when the girls were alone in her room away from anyone who could overhear them.

It was a decorator's dream of a room, done in royal blue and gold. There were twin beds in it, a huge sofa, two comfortable chairs, a desk, and even a loveseat. The gold silk curtains matched the bedspreads which were monogrammed in royal blue.

"Your parents certainly like this color scheme," Trixie said without thinking. "Even their matches—" She stopped, biting her lip.

"It's all right," Di said, smiling. "Honey told me everything last night. About your visit to Hawthorne Street and the package of our matches which that awful man who owns the hotel had in his pocket. But that isn't why I'm sure now that Uncle Monty isn't really my mother's long lost brother."

"Well, what *is* the reason?" Trixie demanded impatiently. "I'm simply dying of curiosity, Di. If Honey told you everything last night, she must have told you that I think the most important clue is in those portraits of your mother's parents."

"There aren't any portraits of my mother's parents," Di said flatly.

"What?" Trixie almost fell off the loveseat. "Why, I was sure I saw portraits of your grandparents when your mother showed me through the gallery last spring. Don't you remember, Di?"

"You did," Di told her. "But let me start at the beginning. After the party Friday night, Uncle Monty locked up the gallery, as Mother had asked him to. But the next morning when the servants wanted to go in there and take down the draperies and clean up the mess, he couldn't find the key. At least, that's what he said. Because we hardly ever use that room, Mother didn't know the key was missing until yesterday afternoon when Honey asked her to show her the gallery. Then Uncle Monty told her that he had misplaced it. That was the word he used. He was sure it would turn up eventually. Mother agreed with him, as she always

does. But just then Dad came home and when he heard the key was missing he had a fit. He sent for a locksmith at once and ordered him to change the locks on both doors.

"While that was going on, the housekeeper and one of the maids began taking down the draperies. Because Dad was so worried for fear some dishonest person had found the key, he made them uncover the valuable paintings first. Eventually they got around to the drapery with the big bat on it and when they took it down, Mother screamed. Because, you see, Trixie," Di finished, "someone had slashed the pictures from their frames!"

Trixie rested her elbows on her knees and cupped her chin in her hands. "I feel like screaming myself," she moaned.

"I don't," Di said. "It was the proof I needed to make me realize that Uncle Monty isn't my uncle. Because, of course, it was he who did it."

"Do your parents suspect Uncle Monty?" Trixie asked hopefully.

"Oh, no," Di told her. "They think someone found the key after Uncle Monty lost it."

"But that doesn't make sense," Trixie pointed out. "If a thief got hold of the key he would have stolen the valuable paintings."

"That's the point," Di agreed. "But Uncle Monty's theory is that the thief planned to steal them all but was interrupted."

"How is this thief supposed to have got in and out of your house?" Trixie demanded.

"Oh, everyone thinks it must have been one of the servants," Di explained. "Or one of the caterers or a member of the orchestra. A lot of people had a chance to steal the portraits on Halloween when the gallery was wide open. Why, even the decorators could have done it. That's why Dad didn't notify the police. How could they ever find the thief now?"

"It's too late for clues," Trixie agreed. "And there are too many suspects. We'll have to find the portraits, that's all, and somehow we'll have to prove that it was Uncle Monty who took them."

"But where are we going to look?" Di wanted to know. "Uncle Monty wouldn't keep them. He must have destroyed them by now."

"Big oil paintings on heavy canvas," Trixie said, "aren't so easy to destroy. When do you suppose he cut them from the frames?"

"I have no idea," Di said.

"*I* have," Trixie cried. "He must have done it right after your father sent for a locksmith. Until the doors were opened, Monty didn't have to worry about the

177

portraits. He knew I wanted to look at them, but he'd fixed things so I wouldn't have a chance to."

"That's right," Di agreed. "If it hadn't been for Honey asking to be shown the gallery, Dad might not have known the key was missing for weeks. And I remember now, Trixie, while we were all in the study waiting for the locksmith to arrive, Uncle Monty disappeared. He said he was going up to his room to have one last look for the key. His room is right above the study and the floor isn't carpeted. If he had gone up there I would have heard him moving around, but I didn't. I wasn't suspicious then, so I didn't think much about it." She clasped her knees excitedly. "What probably happened is this. Instead of going upstairs, he left the house by the front door and sneaked into the gallery from the doors that open on to the terrace. The same key fits both locks. That way, nobody inside the house would have heard or seen him. And, Trixie," she finished, "when the locksmith arrived, it was Uncle Monty who let him into the house through the French doors in the dining room that open on to the terrace."

"M-m-m," Trixie said thoughtfully. "I wonder what he did with the portraits after he cut them out of their frames. If the locksmith arrived while he was sneaking out of the gallery with them, he didn't have time to hide them in his room. Oh, I know!" Trixie jumped up. "The fireplace on the terrace! That's the most logical place. Come on, Di. Let's go look."

"Why?" Di settled back on the loveseat. "What good are some charred scraps going to do us?"

"They might not all be charred," Trixie said. "Besides, how do you know they're scraps? You can't tear canvas, and he wouldn't have dared waste time cutting them up. I think he just crammed them under the logs and set a match to them. And he certainly didn't dare stand around for a long time to make sure they were burned to ashes. So there's a good chance whole sections of the faces may still be intact. The eyes, for instance."

"I think you read too many mysteries," Di said. "In radio and TV shows, detectives are always finding valuable clues in fireplaces. But things like that don't happen in real life."

"Oh, yes, they do," Trixie argued. "If you ever read the papers you'd discover that criminals are often convicted on bits of glass or cloth—even charred scraps of evidence. Please, Di, let's go look now."

"We can't," Di said. "The TV set is on the terrace, and Uncle Monty is glued to it. There are several programs which he wouldn't miss for anything in the world. One is on now. The others are in the evening."

She laughed. "It's driving Dad absolutely crazy. Since Uncle Monty arrived he hasn't been able to listen to any of his own favorite programs. That's why he ordered a set for Uncle Monty, and is having it installed in the *Robin* tomorrow. He's already given Uncle Monty the trailer, you know."

"But why?" Trixie asked, chuckling. "Isn't this huge house big enough for both your father and your so-called uncle?"

"I guess I forgot to tell you about the check," Di said. "Dad just can't stand having Uncle Monty around any longer. As soon as he can sell some bonds, he's going to give him fifty thousand dollars so he can go and do whatever it is he keeps saying he wants to do way out on the coast."

Trixie gasped. "We can't let that happen, Di. When will your father sell those bonds?"

"I don't know," Di said. "I guess it depends on what the stock market does, although I really think Dad wouldn't mind taking a big loss if it meant getting rid of Uncle—I mean Monty. Dad didn't say anything to me about it. I heard him tell Mother. I don't know how she feels about Monty going away, but I know she's awfully glad Dad's going to give him all that money."

"We've got to prove that he's an impostor before that happens," Trixie said. "Can't you ask your mother

180

what color her parents' eyes were, Di?"

"I did ask her," Di said. "The first chance I got last night when Monty wasn't hovering around. She doesn't know. They both died when she was a baby."

"But the portraits," Trixie said. "She must have seen them hundreds of times."

"Mother was so upset," Di said, "I didn't dare mention the portraits."

"Well, *you* must have seen them dozens of times," Trixie said.

Diana shrugged. "I know, but it's a funny thing about eyes. People don't notice the color too much. As many times as I've seen Honey, I thought her eyes were brown until yesterday. And she thought, just because I have black hair, that my eyes were black, too. But they're not. They're violet."

"I guess I notice things like that more than most people," Trixie said rather smugly.

"Is that so?" Di demanded. "What color eyes does our bus driver have? I asked Honey the same question yesterday, and she had no idea."

Trixie grinned ruefully. "Neither have I." Then struck by an idea, she asked, "Di, hasn't your mother some old family records which would tell what color her parents' eyes were? Passports, driver's licenses, and things like that?"

"I guess so," Di said vaguely. "There's a funny little old trunk in the attic filled with keepsakes. But we won't find any passports, or driver's licenses. My grandparents were very poor, you know."

"Maybe we'll find birth certificates then," said Trixie. "Let's go."

The girls spent the rest of the afternoon searching the contents of the battered little trunk. They pored over photographs, diaries, letters, birth certificates, and receipted bills, but nothing gave them the information they wanted. While they were repacking the trunk, Trixie asked, "What about Uncle Monty? Won't he think it's funny when he sees me at dinner this evening?"

"No," Di explained. "I told him that we'd made up because you'd apologized. It was a lie, of course, but I guess it takes a liar to catch a liar."

Trixie laughed. "Just to keep you from being a liar, I will apologize."

"I'm the one who ought to apologize to you," Di said. "I wouldn't have believed the things Uncle Monty said you said if I hadn't thought that he was my mother's own brother."

Trixie suddenly reached out and clamped her hand over Di's mouth. "Sh-h," she whispered, "I think someone's sneaking up the stairs." In a loud voice she said, "I've never had a nicer time. I love to explore attics.

Don't you, Di? I mean, why wait for a rainy day to explore attics when you can do it any day?"

"That's just the way I feel," Di said in an equally loud voice. "Attics should be explored any time you feel like it. Don't you agree, Trixie?"

Both girls carefully avoided looking toward the stairs which were now creaking. "I certainly do," Trixie said. "I've heard of people finding valuable things like stamps and antiques in attics. I could use something valuable right now. I owe Mart a dollar. Seventy-five cents for the cab, and a quarter for taking care of Bobby, you know, when I was supposed to."

Di had no idea what Trixie was talking about but she said vehemently, "You're so right, Trixie. What do you think about that old chair over there? Of course, it's broken, but it just might be an antique." The creaking sounds began to die away.

But to be on the safe side, Trixie kept the conversation going until she was sure that the eavesdropper was out of earshot. Then she said in a low voice, "I'll bet it was Uncle Monty."

"Who else?" Di asked. "And I'm awfully afraid he heard what I said about him. Oh, Trixie, I'm scared. What will he do to me now that he knows I think he's an impostor and not my real uncle?"

"Nothing," Trixie said, closing the little trunk and

starting for the stairs. When they were back in Di's room she added, "He didn't do anything to me, and he's known what I think of him since I tried to look at the portraits at the Halloween party."

"He tried right away to break up our friendship," Di pointed out. "That's about all he could do to you. But I live right here in the house with him." She shivered, just thinking about it.

"I'm living in the house with him at the moment, too," Trixie said, smiling.

Di brightened. "That's an idea. Why don't you keep right on staying with us over the weekend? I wouldn't be scared if you slept in my room with me at night. Please, Trixie, say you will."

"I'd like to," Trixie said. "But I don't think Moms would let me. Not unless your mother called her and said she wanted me an awful lot, and all that sort of thing. And I haven't any clothes. Of course, Brian and Mart could bring me some tomorrow on the school bus."

"Of course they could," Di cried enthusiastically. "I'll go and ask my mother to call your mother right now." She darted off, and Trixie stood in the middle of the room staring unseeingly out of the window.

What would Uncle Monty do if he knew that both girls suspected him? Fifty thousand dollars was an awful lot of money. If he thought they might interfere with his scheme, wouldn't he do everything he could to keep them from exposing him?

Trixie quickly made up her mind. She would examine the contents of the terrace fireplace that very night just as soon as everyone, including Diana, was sound asleep.

14

"I'm Not Afraid!"

IT'S ALL SET," Di said when she came back from her mother's room. "Mart's biking in for some reason, but Brian is bringing your suitcase in the station wagon. He was going to drive in anyway so he can pick up your mother's flowers and flower vases at the Garden Club."

"Swell," Trixie said. "So Mart's biking in, huh? I wonder why."

"Is that so unusual?" Di asked. "When we were in grade school Mart used to bike in and out almost every day. Remember?"

Trixie laughed. "That was because he was forever missing the bus." She gave Di a hug. "Oh, Di, spending the night with you is so much fun. Why, it's just like old times, isn't it?"

186

"Almost but not quite," Di said. "Trixie, I hate this big house, and I don't really like this room. It makes me feel as though I were staying in a hotel."

"Now you're being silly, Di," Trixie said. "It's a perfectly beautiful house with perfectly beautiful furnishings. And this room is super."

"I like your room much better, Trixie," Di insisted. "It's so small and cozy with that lovely hooked rug your grandmother made that has all the colors of the rainbow in it, and the twin maple beds with their nice unbleached muslin spreads. At least that's the way I remember it."

"It's just the same," Trixie said, "except that it seems to get smaller every year. I've got so much junk in my closet I have to lean on the door with all my weight before I can close it."

Di giggled. "I still would rather have a small room. And I'd rather live in a small house like yours."

"Listen, Di," Trixie said seriously, "you've got to stop hating being rich. I can see why it's a nuisance having a butler hovering around. And I think it's a shame you practically never see your kid brothers and sisters. But you go around acting as though having a lot of money is something to be ashamed of. Honey and Jim are awfully rich, but you notice it doesn't seem to bother them."

Di nodded. "They're used to it. I suppose I'll get used to it eventually. But right now I can't help thinking that none of the kids in our class at school like me. When we lived on Main Street they used to drop in all the time. I hate living way out here away from everyone on this lonely country road."

"The road we live on is pretty lonely, too," Trixie said, "and it's just as far from the center of town. But, Di, where you live isn't what makes people decide to like you or not like you."

"That's what Honey said," Di admitted. "When I spent the weekend with her and she spent the night with me, we talked a lot after we went to bed. She says that until she met you and Jim she went around being miserable all the time, so of course she wasn't popular with other boys and girls. She says the reason my friends don't come out here is because I don't invite them."

"That's right," Trixie said. "You notice they all came to your Halloween party and had a wonderful time. Take me, for instance," she added with a chuckle, "every time you've asked me I've accepted, haven't I? But I'll bet I never get invited again if I don't get cleaned up before dinner. It's almost eight."

Di frowned at the clock on her desk. "I wish we didn't have to see Uncle Monty. How are we going to

keep our faces from showing what we know and how we feel about him?"

"We'll have to, that's all," Trixie said. "Don't look at me and don't look at Uncle Monty. That'll be the best way."

"I wish we could wear masks," Di said worriedly. "I guess the best thing to do is to pretend that my real face is a mask." She began to practice in front of the mirror. "How's this for a mask, Trixie? Would you say that I had a dead pan?"

Trixie shook with laughter. "With your cheeks sucked in like that and your eyes practically popping out of your head, you look more like a fish. You're going to have a hard time eating with that kind of a frozen face. Me, I'm going to concentrate on the delicious food you always have."

Somehow during dinner they managed to talk and behave just as though Uncle Monty really were Mrs. Lynch's brother. He, in turn, gave no sign that he suspected them of suspecting him. After dinner Trixie found that she couldn't keep her eyes open any longer. She hadn't had nearly enough sleep the night before, and neither had Di.

"Thank goodness we haven't any homework." Trixie yawned as they undressed and climbed into bed. She fell sound asleep almost the minute her head touched the soft pillow.

Because she had gone to sleep so early, she awoke a few hours later. The luminous dial on Di's clock told her that it was twelve-thirty. Trixie slipped out of bed and cautiously opened the door. The house was very quiet. Di had loaned her a warm housecoat and she quickly put it on. Then in her bare feet she tiptoed down the stairs. The halls were dimly lighted but the dining room which she had to pass through in order to get to the terrace was pitch dark. Trixie tried to peer into the darkness, but couldn't even see the outlines of the heavier pieces of furniture.

"I guess I'll have to turn on a light," she said to herself wishing she had a flashlight or candle. "Either that or trip over the furniture in here and wake everyone in the house." Trixie groped along the walls until she found the light switch. The soft click sounded like a deafening crash, and the suddenness of the bright lights that flooded the room and the terrace seemed blinding. For a moment she stood still, not daring to move.

She hadn't been frightened before but her hands trembled as she opened the French doors and crept across the flagstone floor to the fireplace. It seemed as though a thousand pairs of eyes must be watching her.

191

And, except for two huge, clean logs, the fireplace was empty. Then Trixie remembered that there was another fireplace at the other end of the terrace and she hurried over to it. She poked through the ashes and in a few minutes drew out what she had hardly dared to hope she might be lucky enough to find: two tightly rolled canvases which had been crammed under the bottom log. The backs were scorched but only the corners had been burned away.

Trixie hastily unrolled them and, kneeling on the terrace, spread them flat. Two pairs of blue eyes stared up at her!

"What do you think you're doing?"

It was only a whisper but it was uttered so close to Trixie that it sounded like a shout. For a moment she was too surprised to move; then she turned her head and saw that Uncle Monty was standing right behind her. He was fully clothed but even in that terrible moment she noticed that he was wearing sneakers. That explained why he had been able to creep up behind her without making a sound that would have warned her.

Trixie's eyes traveled from his feet to his face. He looked so angry that she opened her mouth to scream, but only a croak came out of her dry throat.

He grabbed her arm and jerked her roughly to her

feet. "Scream," he hissed, "and I'll—"

Trixie found her voice then. She was much more angry than she was frightened. "Keep your hands off me," she said. "I have no intention of screaming. I'm not afraid of you."

He pointed to the portraits which were slowly rolling up again. "So it was you who committed the vandalism," he whispered hoarsely. "I thought so. That's what you were doing when I caught you in the gallery all alone on Halloween."

Trixie gulped. If anyone came downstairs now and found them on the terrace with those incriminating portraits, it would be Monty's word against hers.

"If you know what's good for you," he continued, "you'll go back to bed and pretend this little scene was a nightmare."

Trixie tossed her head. "While you finish burning the portraits, I suppose? That's what you came downstairs to do, didn't you? It's too bad you didn't have a chance to make sure they were completely burned last night when you slashed them from their frames."

He glared at her. "Little girls who frequent Hawthorne Street shouldn't make a habit of asking impertinent questions."

"So you know about that?" Trixie asked coolly. "Do you also know that I happened to notice that your friend Olyfant had a package of the Lynches' personalized book matches? Maybe you can tell me how he got them. Or how you happened to know I was on Hawthorne Street."

He ignored her questions. "The fact that you were seen on Hawthorne Street can only mean one thing. You were contacting a fence so you could sell those portraits. If Mr. Lynch knew as much about you as I do he wouldn't allow you to speak to his daughter."

Trixie's heart sank. More than ever now she wished she had never gone near Hawthorne Street. She had got a clue but it was one she would never be able to use. In fact, everything she had done so far in order to prove that this man was an impostor could be twisted and turned to be used against her.

She could tell by the mean expression in his small brown eyes that he knew she was helpless. That made Trixie mad. Disdainfully she touched the portraits with her bare toe. "Oh, go ahead and burn them," she said airily. "They don't mean a thing. If you'll notice the signature of the artist, you'll see that he is one of the most famous portrait painters in America. I happen to know about him because he painted Mrs. Wheeler's portrait. He's a very young man, Uncle Monty, and must have been born a long time after Mrs. Lynch's parents died."

He stared at her in chagrined amazement.

"I don't know why we both didn't realize in the beginning," Trixie continued, "that those portraits were done from photographs. Mrs. Lynch's family was very poor. Poor people can't afford to have their portraits painted. She must have had them done quite recently and told the artist to give them blue eyes simply because her own are blue." Trixie tossed her head. "So now, Uncle Monty, you don't have to be any more afraid of me than I am of you. I *think* you're an impostor, but I have no way of proving it." She swept past him into the dining room thinking, *"Not yet anyway."*

Back in Di's room, safely snuggled under the covers, Trixie lay awake for a long time, trying to think of another way of proving that Uncle Monty was an impostor. "There just has to be some good way to prove it," she thought desperately, "but how?"

15

Too Many Problems!

THE NEXT morning Trixie woke Di up early and told her what had happened on the terrace the night before.

"I think we ought to tell Dad right now," Di said as they dressed for school. "Why, Monty as good as confessed to you that he *is* an impostor."

Trixie shook her head. "No, he didn't. I hoped he'd say something that would give us a clue to who he really is, but all he did was threaten me."

Diana shivered. "He's a horrid man. Let's have breakfast in the nursery with the twins so we won't have to look at him."

"That would be fun," Trixie said. "I haven't seen them since they were babies. But will the nurses let us?"

"They had better," Di said firmly. "I'm sick and

196

tired of being bossed by servants. Honey is very polite to the people who work on her place, but you notice she doesn't let them make her life miserable."

Trixie chuckled. In a short time Honey had done wonders! Di was already well on the road to becoming her usual cheerful self. "Honey is just about perfect," Trixie said to Di as they hurried down the hall toward the nursery wing. "I love her."

"I do, too," Di said. "And that's one reason why I hate Monty. He heard me telling Dad and Mother about how Honey is just getting over being scared of spiders and snakes. He doesn't want Honey to like me. That's why he planted all those awful things around at the party. That's also why he tried to make Regan mad. He pretends to like my friends, but you notice he's always trying to break up my friendships."

Trixie nodded. "Well, he'll be gone soon. And that's what worries me. Today is Friday. Suppose your father gives him that check tomorrow? He'll drive off with the trailer and nobody will ever hear of him again."

"I know," Di agreed. "That's why you ought to tell Dad right away what you know about Monty."

"I can't," Trixie moaned. "Not without getting into a lot of trouble. I did sneak into the gallery on Halloween. Before that Harrison saw me swipe a candle

197

from the dining room. He doesn't know why I took it, but don't you see? If your father starts asking a lot of questions, it would surely look as though I was the one who cut the portraits out of the frames."

They had a delicious breakfast in the sunny nursery with the twins who, Trixie decided, were almost as cute and mischievous as Bobby. In spite of the nurses, the little boys and girls managed to spill their cocoa and drop several pieces of French toast on the floor. They were all four quarreling happily when Trixie and Di left.

Because the girls had got up so early it was only seven-thirty when they returned to Di's room. "I think we ought to have a meeting of the Bob-Whites this afternoon," Trixie said suddenly, "and decide what to do about Monty."

"I agree with you," Di said. "Could we have the meeting here? Brian can drive the others home afterwards."

"All right," Trixie said. "I've sort of lost interest in the clubhouse now that it's not really ours any more. But what if Monty hangs around?"

"He won't," Di told her. "He's going in to New York this afternoon to get the tow car Dad bought him. And Harrison won't hang around either. I'm going to tell him that if we get hungry we'll use some of the things

I bought for the Halloween party. We'll have toasted marshmallows and popcorn, so there won't be any reason for him to come near us with his silly old silver tray."

"Great," Trixie said with a grin. "I'll call Honey now and tell her to notify the others so our parents won't expect anybody home until late this afternoon."

When Trixie finished telephoning, the girls went downstairs and found that Mr. Lynch was just about to leave for the station in the limousine.

"I'll drop you kids off at the school if you're all set," he said cheerfully.

"Oh, that would be wonderful," Trixie said gratefully. "It's a long walk to the bus stop at the end of your driveway."

"Almost a mile," he agreed as they climbed into the back seat of the car. "That's why I'd like to take Di to school every day, but she isn't usually up and ready so early."

"That's not true!" Di affectionately hugged her father's arm. "You're the one who's lazy in the morning. If I waited for you, I'd be late to school every day."

Mr. Lynch chuckled. "It's the truth. I got up early this morning so I wouldn't have the pleasure of riding in to New York on the train with your uncle. He planned to take the nine-fifteen with me, so I just decided that I'd take the eight-forty-five." His big shoulders shook with laughter. "Well, here you are, girls."

They waved good-bye and hurried up the steps to the school. "Your father doesn't like Monty any more than we do," Trixie said. "Oh, I can't wait until we prove that he is an impostor."

"And I," Di said, "can't wait for the gang to get together at our house this afternoon."

They held the meeting on the terrace at four o'clock. Trixie did most of the talking and for once the boys listened without interrupting. They frowned at her darkly when she described her visit to the hotel on Hawthorne Street, but said nothing until she had finished telling them about her scene with Uncle Monty the night before.

Then Jim said soberly, "Well, he's a crook all right. I think, Trix, you ought to tell the whole story to Mr. Lynch as soon as he comes home."

"I do, too," Brian agreed.

"Well, I don't," Mart said. "We haven't got a shred of proof. We can't drag Tom into it because we promised not to. So what have we got? Matches and portraits! Do you think Mr. Lynch is going to believe that Trixie actually went to Skid Row? Or that she

found the portraits under those logs? Or that she had
that fantastic chat with Uncle Monty out here last
night? We believe her because we know that she's
crazy enough to take all sorts of chances when she's
tracking down a mystery. But Mr. Lynch will simply
think she's crazy. Period. Full stop."

"I agree with Mart," Honey said. "How do you feel
about it, Di? You know your father better than the
rest of us. Would he believe Trixie?"

"I don't think so," Di said. "But it might make him
suspicious enough to hire private detectives."

"What's the matter with us?" Mart demanded.
"We're supposed to be amateur detectives. By the time
private dicks get going on the case, Uncle Monty will
have faded into anonymity."

"Into what?" Di asked.

Mart waved his hands. "Namelessness. Thin air.
Once he's cashed that check, no one will ever hear
of Montague Wilson again."

"Not unless there's a real Montague Wilson," Trixie
pointed out.

"Which I very much doubt," Mart said. "I mean, not
alive. If he is alive, why didn't he get in touch with his
sister long ago?"

"He probably tried to," Di said, "but didn't get
anywhere. When my grandparents died, the welfare

people put my mother in a foster home. She used her foster parents' last name until she married Dad. So, as far as my real uncle knew, *she* vanished while she was still a baby."

"True," Mart said, "but last spring your whole family history appeared in both newspapers and magazines. If he's alive, your uncle must have seen one of those stories."

"The Monty we know saw them all right," Trixie said. "My theory is that he met the real Monty out west somewhere about the same time those stories were published. Di's uncle is probably a very nice person and didn't want to get in touch with his sister then, after all those years, because it would look as though he hadn't cared anything about her until her husband made a million dollars. So the Monty we know decided to impersonate him. But he didn't know enough about Mrs. Lynch to convince her that he was her brother. So he came east and scouted around until he finally found that Olyfant was the man who could give him the information he needed."

"That makes sense," Brian agreed. "I've been wondering why Monty risked going back to Hawthorne Street after he showed up at the Lynches'. The answer is, of course, that he went back to pay Olyfant for the information."

"But he hasn't got the money from Mr. Lynch yet," Jim put in. "Has he, Di?"

Di shook her head. "Mother gives him spending money, but she never has very much because she charges practically everything. Oh!" She dropped the marshmallow she had been toasting into the fire. "That explains the birds."

Mart groaned. "The plot thickens. What birds?"

"The china ones in the study," Di explained. "It's a very valuable collection, but each bird alone is worth about a thousand dollars. The last time I looked at them I thought two or three were missing but since I've never counted them I couldn't be sure. Now I *am* sure," she finished, "and I'm going to tell Dad the minute he comes home."

"That won't do any good," Trixie said. "You can't prove that Monty stole them. Even the police would have a hard time proving that. The birds could have been broken or stolen during the Halloween party."

"Let's get back to Olyfant," Honey interrupted. "How did he happen to have the information Monty wanted?"

"There are records at the county courthouse, and he could have got a lot of dope from back numbers of *The Sleepyside Sun*." Jim patted Honey's hand. "You're too young and innocent to understand the nature of shady characters like Olyfant. They make it their business to know all there is to know about rich or famous people like the Lynches."

"I still don't understand," Honey said. "Newspapers and county clerks don't give information to just anyone, especially not to shady characters."

"But crooked politicians do," Jim said, grinning.

"That's right," Mart said. "I've been looking into Olyfant. He has been arrested dozens of times, but never convicted of anything. That spells a crooked political connection in capital letters."

Trixie leaned across Honey to tap Mart's knee. *"You* have been looking into Olyfant? I thought you were of the opinion that Tom was talking through his hat the other night when he said he saw Uncle Monty at the station."

"Not me," Mart said. "Tom taught Brian and me how to fish and shoot. We used to tag along after him when we were Bobby's age. I can't remember when I didn't know that he had a photographic memory. Once he's traveled over a route he can tell you every single landmark on it, and he never forgets a face."

"That's absolutely true," Brian agreed. "And it's why Tom makes such a good chauffeur. One reason. Another is that he's as honest as the day is long."

"I know," Honey and Jim said in the same voice.

Jim added, "I don't know why I was dumb enough to think that Tom had made a mistake about Uncle Monty." He clutched his red hair with both hands. "Wishful thinking, I suppose. I couldn't bear the thought of Trixie dragging us right back into another mystery so soon after the last one was solved."

"Same here," Brian said with a rueful chuckle. "But now I *am* in the mood for a mystery. And I think that under the circumstances, since time is of the essence, it's up to us to prove Uncle Monty is an impostor before he makes off with all that money."

"He won't be able to cash that check in a hurry," Jim said thoughtfully. "How's he going to live in the meantime?"

"Easy," Mart said. "He'll sell the *Robin* right off. It would only handicap him in more ways than one. *A*, it would make him stick out like a sore thumb if Mr. Lynch should put dicks on his trail. *B,* it would slow down his speed."

"I don't agree with you," Trixie put in. "That trailer is a perfect little home on wheels. It's got a darling little kitchenette and a bathroom with a separate shower compartment. Besides, it's a very attractive combination living room and bedroom. And now it even has a TV set. I don't think Uncle Monty would sell it in a hurry. Why should he? What's he got to fear from Mr.

Lynch? Nobody suspects him except us."

"If he does sell it," Honey said more to herself than to the others, "I wish he'd sell it to Tom. It would make a perfect home for him and Celia. Daddy would give them a nice plot of land."

"More wishful thinking," Jim said. "Where would Tom get the money for a trailer?"

"I don't know," Honey admitted. "But it's going to cost them an awful lot of money to put a bathroom and a kitchen in the gatehouse. Not to mention laying floors. I can't imagine why Celia has her heart set on our clubhouse. It's perfect for us, but I think she's going to end up hating it. And so does Miss Trask."

"The main reason why Celia likes it," Jim explained, "is because it's on our property. If they set up house-keeping in the village, they'll lose their jobs because Dad and Mother have to have a maid and a chauffeur who live on the premises. The gatehouse is the obvious place, and there's nothing we can do about it. So let's get back to Uncle Monty. Trixie's right. He's not going to sell the *Robin*. It would make a perfect hideout if he ever should need one. All he has to do is park it in the woods beside a stream, first having stocked it with canned goods."

"Without electricity," Mart objected, "it's nothing more than a little house on wheels, and an awfully conspicuous one. Monty knows Trix suspects him. He can't be sure that she won't tell Mr. Lynch what she knows. Maybe not right away, but eventually. If I were in his shoes, I'd get rid of that trailer as soon as I cashed the check."

"Well, you're not in his shoes," Trixie argued. "And I don't think he's the least bit afraid of me. And even if he is, I agree with Jim. The trailer would make a perfect hideout."

"Oh, let's not argue," Honey wailed. "I feel so discouraged about everything. All my life I dreamed about belonging to a secret club and having a secret clubhouse, and then just when we get things all set, ping! The bubble bursts. There's no sense in our sitting around here talking about Uncle Monty. There isn't a single solitary thing we can do about him."

"I feel discouraged, too," Di said. "Why don't we just let him go? Dad won't miss the money."

"We can't do that," Trixie said. "It would amount to practically the same thing as aiding and abetting a criminal, wouldn't it?"

"But we really don't know whether or not he is a criminal," Di said.

"I'm going to know pretty soon," Trixie said.

"How?" everyone asked her at once.

"Never mind," she replied mysteriously. "If I don't

have proof by tomorrow morning that Uncle Monty is a criminal, you can chop off my head."

"Nobody wants your head," Mart said. "It looks quite nice on your shoulders. But without the rest of you—no thanks." He shuddered elaborately.

"Shut up, Mart," Brian said sternly. "This is no time to joke about corpses. If Trixie isn't careful, she'll end up as one."

"That's right," Jim added. "People have committed murder for less than fifty grand. You stay out of this, Trix. All of you girls stay out of it. Brian and Mart and I will get the proof we need."

"I intend to stay out of it," Di said emphatically. "I'm scared of Uncle Monty."

"Me, too," Honey admitted. "If he'd caught *me* out on this terrace in the dead of night, I know I'd have dropped dead on the spot."

"Let's drop death from the conversation," Trixie said with a chuckle. "Impostors don't murder people. They're borderline crooks and are very careful not to do anything which might land them in jail."

"Don't be too sure of that, Sis," Mart said, drawing his finger across Trixie's throat. "Most crooks will cross the border for fifty grand. Now, *I* have a plan which will get us all the proof we need without endangering our lives in any way whatsoever."

209

"What is it?" Trixie demanded sourly. "Something simple, I'll bet. Such as, kidnaping him and torturing him until he confesses. Our clubhouse is just the place. No one will hear his screams." She got up and bowed. "Allow me to be the first to congratulate you, Mastermind. I knew you'd think of something."

Mart returned the bow. "Thank you, Genius. How did you read my mind? That's exactly what I plan to do: Force a confession from him."

"I give up," Brian said with disgust. "If you two are going to clown around, we won't accomplish anything. I move that this meeting be closed."

"I second the motion," said Jim. "Come on, kids, let's go. Brian and I will think of something that makes sense."

"All right, Brains," Mart said, leading the way out of the terrace, "but let me get my bike out of the station wagon before you depart. Don't expect me again until you see me."

"You'd better be home for dinner," Brian said.

"Not so," Mart returned. "I have parental permission to partake of nourishment in the village this evening and to spend the night with a classmate who really is a brain and who is coaching me in that most difficult of all subjects, math."

Trixie and Di followed them out to the garage where

Brian had parked the station wagon beside the huge red trailer. Mart took his bicycle from the back, then the others drove off. He stared at the *Robin* with a curious expression on his freckled face.

"What's the matter with you?" Trixie demanded. "One would think you'd never seen a trailer before."

"I've never been inside that one," Mart said. "And I'd like to, since if it had not been for it, you and Honey might never have found Jim." He turned to Di. "I suppose it's locked?"

"Oh, no," Di said, opening the nearest door. She reached inside and turned on the overhead lights. "Go on in, Mart. Look around as long as you like."

He went in and came out again in a few minutes. "A veritable palace on wheels," he said. "Does the TV set work?"

"It had better," Di told him. "Two of Monty's favorite programs are on this evening. One at nine and one at eleven. Two of Dad's favorites are on at the same time, but they're not the same ones."

"Such luxury," Mart said, sighing. "Such luxury. So cozy. I imagine Monty stays out here in between programs?"

"No," Di said. "He and Mother sandwich canasta in between. They're both fiends."

Mart grinned. "Monty is a fiend, but your mother is

an angel." He got on his bike and pedaled off down the driveway.

Trixie stared after him thoughtfully. "Mart is up to something," she said to Di as they started back toward the terrace. "I wish I knew what it was. If only I hadn't kidded him about his plan! If I hadn't, he might have told me what it was!"

16

Just One Chance!

JUST THEN a brand new coupé appeared on the drive-way. "Here comes Monty now," Di said to Trixie. "Oh, Dad's with him. I guess they must have met somewhere in New York and decided to come out together."

They watched as Monty parked the car near the steps to the terrace. Both men got out, waved to the girls, and went inside the house.

"That's queer," Trixie said. "I thought your father hated the sight of Monty."

"He does," Di said. "Why else do you suppose he had a TV set installed in the *Robin?*"

"Then why didn't he come home by train as he usually does?" Trixie asked. "I shouldn't think he would have enjoyed driving from New York with someone he despises that much."

Di frowned. "Dad looked awfully cheerful, too, didn't he? He usually looks as though he had a tummy-ache when he's in the same room with Monty. Let alone in the same car."

"There can be only one answer," Trixie moaned. "Your father's happy about the whole thing because he knows Monty is leaving soon. And that means Monty must have the check in his wallet right now."

"That suits me fine," Di said as they strolled toward the terrace steps. "I hope he leaves right after we're finished eating dinner."

"I don't think he'll leave tonight," Trixie said thoughtfully. "But if he has got the check, he'll leave first thing in the morning. It's not much fun driving at night in a brand new tow car with a trailer."

Trixie's theory proved to be correct. Hardly were they all seated at the dining-room table when Mr. Lynch said to Di with undisguised joy: "Your uncle is driving back to the far, far west tomorrow morning, dear. *Early* tomorrow morning. So be sure to say good-bye to him this evening. He wants to avoid the traffic on the highway, so he'll be gone before we are awake."

Staring into her soup, Di said dutifully, "Good-bye, Uncle Monty."

Mr. Lynch roared with laughter, but Mrs. Lynch

gasped. "Diana!" she cried in a horrified tone of voice. "Couldn't you wait until just before you go to bed? *Really,* darling. And you must remember to give your precious uncle a farewell kiss."

The thought of kissing Uncle Monty made Diana shudder, and Trixie shuddered sympathetically.

"Fond embraces are not necessary," Mr. Lynch said to his wife. "The child hardly knows your brother. And since the chances are good that she will never see him again, I see no reason for a sentimental scene."

Mrs. Lynch's lower lip trembled. "My own brother, my only brother, my long lost big brother—"

Monty patted her plump hand and said soothingly, "It's all right, Sister. I know I am not popular with your husband and your daughter, although I have striven to please them in every way. They have never returned my affection, but I forgive them from the depth of my heart. Your husband has been most generous in giving me such a large endowment fund for my boys' school. I am very grateful to him."

"Well, I'm glad there are no hard feelings, Monty," Mr. Lynch said with a jovial smile.

Trixie didn't pay much attention to the rest of the conversation; she was too busy thinking. Monty was leaving early the next morning. After that, it would be too late to prove that he was an impostor. Once he got away, even if she could prove it, Monty could be as far away as South America for all she knew. Trixie looked over toward Uncle Monty. He was smiling at something Mrs. Lynch had said and seemed strangely satisfied with himself. Suddenly, Trixie made up her mind. She would search Monty's room for clues that very night. And somehow she had to get hold of a flashlight.

After dinner the girls went straight up to Di's room. Trixie unpacked the suitcase which Brian had carried upstairs earlier. Pretending to be very sleepy, she quickly donned a pair of flannel pajamas and slipped into bed. "Good night, Di," she said, feeling a little guilty because she hadn't shared her plan with her hostess. But how could she? Di herself had admitted twice that she was afraid of Monty.

"Good night, Trixie," Di said, and turned out the bedside light.

Trixie promptly sat up. "Why, it's as light as day outdoors," she cried. "And it's too overcast for the moon to be shining so brightly."

"It's the floodlights," Di said sleepily. "We usually leave them on until the last car has been put away for the night. It makes it easier to get in and out of the garage, you know." She yawned. "If the light bothers you I'll pull down the shades."

"Oh, no," Trixie said hastily. "I love it." To herself she added, "If you only knew how much I love it." She lay there tensely for what seemed like hours, thinking, "At nine Monty went out to the *Robin* to watch television. At nine-thirty he came back in to play canasta with Mrs. Lynch. It's nine-forty-five. Di is sound asleep. *Now is the time.*"

She slipped out of bed and into the hall. At the top of the stairs she listened to the murmur of voices. Sure enough, Monty and Mrs. Lynch were in the study. Then Trixie hurried on to Monty's room. Somewhere in that room must be the evidence she needed to prove that he was an impostor. There had to be something—a letter, a notebook, a newspaper clipping . . . .

Trixie quietly closed the door behind her and stood there for a minute until her eyes grew accustomed to the dim light. Beside the bed were two suitcases, strapped and locked. Trixie dashed across the room and flung open the closet door. It was empty. The bureau drawers were empty, too, and so were the bed-table drawers. Monty was not going to leave the next morning. He was obviously planning to leave that very night!

Too late Trixie remembered that he was in the study below. He could hardly have helped hearing her as she searched his room, slamming the closet door and

218

the drawers in her haste. Quickly she darted out into the hall. Someone had started up the stairs. Whoever it was would see her if she tried to get back into Di's room. If it was Monty she couldn't hide in his room. If it was Mr. or Mrs. Lynch, she couldn't hide in their room across the hall. And she couldn't stay where she was in the hall. Every avenue of escape seemed to be cut off.

"It has to be Monty," Trixie decided desperately. She streaked across the hall into Di's parents' room, softly closing the door in the nick of time. She leaned against it, holding her breath as she listened to the footsteps. Someone went into Monty's room, came right out again, and went back downstairs.

Trixie let out a long sigh of relief and tiptoed to the banister. The murmur of voices told her that Monty and Mr. and Mrs. Lynch were all in the study. Trixie couldn't even guess how long Monty would stay there, but she knew that if she was ever going to get the evidence she needed to prove that he was an impostor, she would have to search the *Robin* for clues.

It was now or never. Trixie flew down the stairs and left the house by the front door. She raced across the terrace and down the steps to the lawn. When her bare feet hit the graveled driveway she winced with pain but didn't dare stop. Harrison's rooms were in the back of the house and overlooked the garage. If he glanced out of a window he couldn't help seeing her.

Trixie shivered as much from cold as from nervousness. The temperature had dropped about fifteen degrees since the sun had gone down, and she wished now that she had put on the warm housecoat which Di had loaned her. By the time she reached the trailer step, her teeth were chattering and her hands were so numb she thought at first the door was locked. As she struggled with the handle her heart suddenly jumped into her throat for she heard a click inside.

"No one's in there," she told herself sternly. "Monty couldn't possibly have got here ahead of you, and he's the only one who ever uses the trailer. It must have been the electric clock."

Then the handle gave and she forced herself to step inside. It was gray darkness in the trailer and the light from outside cast strange black shadows on the walls. Trixie felt her heart beating faster.

Suddenly Trixie laughed at herself. "If I'm ever going to find any clues, I'll have to turn on the light." She felt along the wall for the switch and turned it on. Then she opened the trailer door again. "Just in case I have to leave in a hurry," Trixie told herself.

Ready to begin her search now, Trixie glanced around the room. She decided to go into the kitchenette to make sure no one was lurking in there. Then she opened the closet. In it was Monty's topcoat and she immediately forgot everything else as she searched the pockets. In an inside pocket she found a little black notebook which was held together with rubber bands.

Trixie yanked the rubber bands off, and a piece of pink paper fell to the floor. Even before she picked it up she realized that it was a pistol license. In one corner of it was a photograph of Monty, but the name of the person to whom the license had been issued was not Montague Wilson. In that space on the permit the name Tilney Britten had been neatly typed.

"Drop it!"

Trixie whirled around to face Tilney Britten, alias Monty Wilson, who was standing in the doorway of the *Robin,* a pistol in his hand.

"Drop it," he said again. "Can't you see I've got a gun?"

17

Prisoners!

TRIXIE LET the pistol permit slip from her nerveless fingers. The boys had been right after all. This man was a dangerous criminal. He would stop at nothing. And there was nothing to stop him. Now she remembered something she had only noticed subconsciously before. The new tow car was hitched to the trailer. He could leave right now and take her with him. No one would know she was missing until morning.

Trixie swallowed hard. No matter what happened she was never going to let him know that she was afraid. "So, Mr. Britten," she said, hoping her voice wouldn't betray her, "you are an impostor after all."

He chuckled evilly. "You're too smart for your own good, little girl. Since I'm going to tie your hands

222

behind your back and gag you in a few minutes, I might as well let you do a little talking now. No one will interrupt us. I have said my fond farewells to that silly Mrs. Lynch and her generous husband. Now I'm ready to leave. My suitcases are outside."

"That's why you went upstairs to your room a while ago," Trixie said. "I should have guessed."

"You've got a lot to learn," he said. "It's too bad you aren't going to live long enough to grow up and learn that you should mind your own business."

"Don't be silly," Trixie said. *The thing to do was to stall for time*. Maybe Harrison had seen her. Maybe the prim butler was reporting to Mrs. Lynch right now that her houseguest, wearing nothing but flannel pajamas, had wandered into the garage a few minutes ago. "Don't be silly," she said again, forcing herself to smile. "You're much too smart to harm me in any way, Mr. Britten. You know those portraits don't prove anything and neither did my trip to Hawthorne Street. So you needn't worry. I still haven't got any proof that you're not Mr. Montague Wilson. Not unless you plan to let me depart with that pistol permit, Mr. Britten."

"I'm not going to let you depart at all," he said. "Now that you know my real name, you wouldn't waste any time having me arrested. You can't get a pistol license without being thumb-printed. No matter what name I took after I let you go, the FBI would track me down in a matter of a few hours."

"The FBI will get you anyway," Trixie said, "for kidnaping, if you don't let me go. When the Lynches discover I'm missing tomorrow morning, don't you think they're going to put two and two together to guess what happened to me?"

"They can guess," he said, grabbing Trixie's hands. "By that time I'll be miles away. The Lynches don't know my real name."

Trixie stood passively while he tied her hands behind her back. There was no sense in struggling. "You'll never get a chance to cash that check," she said in order to hide the lump of fright that was rising in her throat. "Try it tomorrow morning and see what happens—see how fast the police nab you."

"What check?" he demanded. "I got cash from Lynch today. After our little conversation on the terrace last night, I decided to take no chances." He took a handkerchief from his pocket, wound it, and tied it tightly across Trixie's mouth.

Trixie sank down on a bunk and blinked to keep from crying. He pulled the draperies, partly covering the side windows, and left the trailer, locking both doors from the outside. Now there was no hope, no chance of rescue. She would have given anything to

see a familiar face—even Bobby's—then.

Bobby! Trixie let the tears come. Would she ever see him or her mother or father or any of her brothers again? Then the lights went out and the darkness made the situation intolerable. The motor of the tow car started up and in another minute the *Robin* was bumping out of the garage and into the light again. At the same moment Trixie saw out of the corner of one eye that the door to the shower compartment was slowly, slowly opening. If she could have screamed she would have screamed at the top of her lungs. And then to her amazement and joy, a familiar freckled face appeared in the crack. The boy who came out of the shower compartment was Mart Belden!

They were in darkness suddenly for the trailer had left the pool of the floodlights. But thank goodness, Mart had a flashlight. He clicked it on with one hand and yanked the handkerchief from her face with the other.

"Oh, Mart," was all Trixie could say.

"Take it easy, kid," he said gently as he freed her hands. "Don't worry, we'll get out of this scrape. And when we do get out, I'm going to be sure to black both of that guy's eyes."

"B-But how did you get in the shower compartment?" Trixie asked weakly.

226

"Never mind that now," Mart said. "I was about to appear on the scene earlier but when I heard Monty say he had a gun I realized I had better stay put. Otherwise I'd be in the same fix you were, and we would both have been helpless." As he spoke he opened the windows on both sides of the trailer.

They had left the Lynch estate and were traveling along the deserted river road. Trixie jumped up to peer out of the back window, hoping against hope that she might glimpse the headlights of an approaching car.

"Oh, Mart," she cried. "Why didn't you yell as we passed the Lynches' house? Someone there might have heard you."

He shook his head. "With the doors and windows closed, the only someone would have been Monty. And don't forget he's got a gun, Trixie. And he won't hesitate to use it either. This escape of Monty's is the last step in his scheme to get money from the Lynches. He's not going to let us stop him now. Remember that, Trix."

Now that she was no longer alone and helpless, Trixie began to recover her spirits. "I'm not likely to forget it," she said tartly. "But, Mart, suppose he sticks to back roads? What are we going to do?"

Mart pulled off his sweater and handed it to her.

227

"You're shivering with cold," he said, "and haven't got sense enough to know it." As he helped her slip it on he added, "About five miles from here, this road merges with Main Street at the intersection to the highway. Unless it's his night off, Spider Webster will be on duty. If the light is red, Monty will have to stop and we can yell out of the window. If it's green, we've somehow got to attract Spider's attention as we pass him."

Trixie nodded. "But how?"

"That I don't know," Mart admitted. "I just keep hoping the light will be red and at that point my mind goes blank."

"I know what we can do," Trixie cried. "There are lots of pots and pans in the kitchenette. We can throw them at Spider. That'll make him so mad he'll surely jump on his motorcycle and go after the driver of the tow car. *If,* as you say, he's on duty."

"Any cop will do," Mart said. "You've got a brain, Sis. And boy, will it ever be fun to throw things and not get arrested for it."

Trixie grinned. "I just hope whatever I throw lands near enough to Spider to attract his attention." She stopped suddenly. "Mart! Suppose nobody's on duty at the intersection?"

"There's just got to be," Mart said grimly. "There always is."

"Yes," Trixie said, "but suppose he's gone off after a car that was traveling too fast or a car that ignored the traffic light?"

"That can't happen to us," Mart said. "And if it does, when we get on the highway we can attract the attention of a passing car."

"I doubt that," Trixie said. "They whiz by in both directions. And it's night. If it were daytime we could yell and wave something out of the back window." Then, as she was struck by a horrible thought, Trixie grabbed the flashlight from Mart and turned it off.

"What's the matter with you—" he began.

"The front window," she gasped. "Suppose Monty should look back and see a light in here."

They almost knocked each other down in their haste to close that window and draw the blind. Trixie turned on the flashlight and Mart collapsed on a bunk, mopping his brow.

"Gleeps," he moaned, catching his breath. "Why didn't I think of that?"

Then, to their horror, they realized that they were hardly moving at all. Monty must have seen the light after all, and was slowly easing the car and trailer to a stop on one side of the road!

"Quick!" Trixie whispered, handing Mart the rope with which Monty had tied her hands. "I'll gag myself.

229

You tie my hands together—and get back into the shower compartment!"

Mart obeyed orders just in time. Monty, with both gun and flashlight, appeared a split second after the shower door closed. He directed the beam at Trixie, and she was sure he must be able to see and hear the wild beating of her heart. Suppose he decided to look in the shower compartment? What would he do if he discovered Mart? He could so easily bind and gag him, too. He could drag them both off into the woods and leave them there to die slowly from starvation and exposure.

Trixie stared at him, hoping that her eyes looked defiant. He leered. "Thought I saw a light in here. Guess it was the reflection of my own headlights." He backed down the step, closed the door, and locked it. In a minute the trailer was speeding along the road again and Mart came out of the shower compartment.

As he released Trixie he said, "I died a thousand deaths in there. Do you realize the windows, except for the front one, are open now? And when Monty was in here before, they were closed!"

Trixie let out her pent-up breath in a long sigh. "He aimed the flashlight he was carrying at me and at nothing else. I never thought about the windows. All I could think about was that this is a deserted road and he had a gun in his hand."

Mart peered out of a window. "It won't be long now," he said. "We'd better get armed."

"And man the portholes," Trixie said with a nervous giggle as she followed him into the kitchenette. "Let's see. When we reach the intersection, the cop on duty will be on our left. So we'd better man the windows on the left side, huh?"

Mart nodded. "Hold the flashlight while I get our ammunition in place." He stacked pots, pans, and their lids on the bunks underneath two of the windows. Then they sat down to wait.

18

"A Likely Tale!"

IT SEEMED like hours to Trixie as she and Mart crouched on the bunks, waiting tensely. Mart's voice was a croak as he whispered:

"We're moving faster and faster. Have you noticed it? He must plan to shoot through the intersection."

"I hope he shoots through a red light," Trixie said. "He won't get far if he does."

"Not if Spider is on duty," Mart agreed. He grabbed a frying pan with one hand and a coffeepot with the other. "We're almost there, Trix. Ready . . . on your mark . . . get set . . . GO!"

Kneeling on the bunk, Trixie threw her ammunition out of the window wildly. She got only a faint, dizzy glimpse of a policeman as they passed him, and hoped that at least one of the pots she had thrown would land somewhere near him.

Then, without realizing what she was doing she stuck her head out of the window and yelled:

"Help! Help! Spider! Help!"

Mart dragged her back. "Shut up! Don't you realize what a fix we're in if Monty heard you and nobody comes to our rescue?"

And then they heard a shrill whistle and, a moment later, the roar of a motorcycle and the long, drawn-out wail of its siren.

It was Mart who was yelling now, but he stopped after Spider shot past them.

"Pull over, you!" they heard the policeman shout.

The trailer slowed and finally stopped. The roar of the motorcycle sputtered into silence. Trixie took a deep breath and screamed: "Watch out, Spider! He's got a gun."

Without glancing in her direction, the policeman drew his revolver from its holster and said to the driver of the tow car, "What goes on here anyway?"

"I don't know what you mean, officer." Monty climbed out of the coupé, and in the motorcycle headlights, Trixie could see that he was smiling.

"So you don't know?" Spider jerked his thumb over one shoulder. "So there's nothing funny about the

Belden kids yelling and throwing pans at me from the windows of your trailer?"

Monty glanced coolly at Trixie and Mart who were breathlessly hanging as far out of the windows as they could.

"I never saw those kids before," he said with a shrug. "Stowaways, no doubt."

Trixie found her voice then. "He locked us in, Spider. He's got the key. Make him let us out. But get his gun first."

Spider patted Monty's pockets and took his pistol from one of them. "Got a permit to carry this?"

"Why, certainly, officer." Monty handed him the folded piece of pink paper.

Spider glanced at it. "Let the kids out."

With a bored expression on his face, Monty obeyed. Trixie climbed out first. Spider glared at her. "I've seen you in some funny outfits, Trixie Belden, but this one beats 'em all. A sweater that's four sizes too big, pajamas, and bare feet. What do you think this is . . . Halloween? Get back inside and get dressed properly."

"I can't," Trixie wailed. "I haven't any other clothes with me, Spider."

"The child is obviously out of her mind," Monty said. "Now, if you don't mind, I'll go along. I'm sure

you must have notified headquarters from your post before you left it, so a patrol car will be here in a minute or so. They can cope with these problem children."

Mart spoke up then. "Spider, he's a crook of the first water. And I—" He stopped as they heard the siren of the approaching patrol car.

Spider frowned at Mart suspiciously. "You were saying?"

"I can prove it," Mart finished. "Inside the trailer is a wire recording machine. If you'll let me play back the spool that's on it now, you'll see what I mean. It's this guy's confession that he's an impostor, a kidnaper, and—"

"Oh, Mart," Trixie interrupted. "You don't have to tell lies."

"I'm not lying," Mart said. He went back inside the trailer, and as the patrol car stopped behind it, came out with a portable recording machine under one arm.

Trixie was so surprised she sank down weakly on the trailer step. But she could tell that Monty was even more surprised than she was. His face was white and pinched with both fright and anger. One of the two men in the patrol car got out and said to Spider:

"What is this, a picnic?"

Spider shook his head. "It's all beyond me." He pointed to Mart. "I vote we all go inside the trailer and listen to what that spool may have to say."

Mart shook his head. "I can't play it back here. No electricity."

At that Monty pulled himself together. "Don't you see, officers? It's nothing but a childish prank. I never saw either this boy or that girl before. When I locked the doors of my trailer, I didn't know they were hiding inside." He laughed. "A joke's a joke, but, after all, officer, I'm in a hurry, so I'll—"

"Wait a minute," Mart interrupted. "This is not a joke, Spider. When I got that man's confession on this spool, the trailer's current *was* connected. To an outlet in the Lynches' garage."

"Never mind, never mind," Spider said. "I've heard enough of this nonsense." He turned to the other policeman. "Take 'em all to headquarters, Molinson. Maybe the sergeant can find out what this is all about." He got on his motorcycle and drove off.

Trixie stared after him hopelessly. And then she realized that Molinson was staring at *her* curiously. Trixie opened her mouth to explain why she was dressed so peculiarly, but before she could say a word he cried:

"Now I know who you are. Trixie Belden! You were

237

one of the kids who helped us catch those big-time pickpockets last August."

Trixie nodded. "Now I remember you, too, Mr. Molinson. And please, won't you take us all to head-quarters? This man is really a dangerous criminal."

"Let's go," Molinson said, taking Monty's arm. "Come along, kids."

Half an hour later they were all seated in a private room at the police station. Both the sergeant and the lieutenant were there, too. Trixie tried to tell them the story from the very beginning, but Monty kept interrupting so nothing she said made much sense.

"I never saw these kids before," he said for about the fourteenth time.

"You're beginning to sound like a broken record," the lieutenant said impatiently. He made a motion with his hand toward the door, and Molinson tapped Monty on the shoulder, motioning him to leave.

"Come along with me, sir," Molinson said politely. "We'll wait outside at the desk."

After they had gone, Trixie began again. For Tom's sake as well as her own, she left out of the story her visit to Hawthorne Street. When she started to describe how she had sneaked into the trailer when it was parked in the Lynches' garage, and had gone through

238

Monty's pockets, she began to stammer. "W-Well, th-then," she finished, "I-I t-turned around and th-there he was with a g-gun pointed right at me."

"A likely tale," the lieutenant said sarcastically, and turned to Mart. "Okay, son. Plug your machine in that outlet over there. Let's hear what that famous spool you keep mumbling about has to say."

Molinson returned then and stood by the closed door. You could have heard a pin drop in the silence that elapsed while Mart obeyed the lieutenant's orders. Trixie still had no idea how or when the recording machine had got into the *Robin,* so she watched the spool turn without any hope that a sound would come from it.

And then the stillness was broken by Monty's voice. Trixie jumped, sure that he must be somewhere in the room, or that she was reliving that nightmare when he had caught her with the pistol permit.

"Drop it! . . . Drop it. Can't you see I have a gun?" Another deafening silence, and then Trixie's voice, so exactly like her own that everyone turned to look at her:

"So, Mr. Britten, you *are* an impostor after all."

The spool spun out an evil chuckle followed by Monty's threatening voice: "You're too smart for your own good, little girl. Since I'm going to tie your hands behind your back and gag you in a few minutes, I might as well—"

"That's enough," the lieutenant said. "For now anyway." He gestured to Molinson. "The sergeant and I will cope with Mr. Britten. Will you be so kind as to cope with the Beldens?"

"Gladly, sir," Molinson said, grinning. "Shall I dump them in the river, sir, take them home, or give them badges?"

"All three in that order," the lieutenant said sternly, but his eyes were twinkling.

"Just leave me in the river," Trixie said mournfully. "When Moms sees me in these clothes at this hour of night—I mean morning—well, frankly, Lieutenant, I'd rather go to jail."

"That's just what I thought," he said. "The next time you try to capture an armed criminal singlehanded, I hope that you will know enough at least to wear something on your feet."

19

Rewards for Everybody!

ON SATURDAY morning the Bob-Whites met at the clubhouse. The Beldens hadn't had much sleep, what with Trixie and Mart arriving after midnight in a patrol car, and the long explanations that were necessary. Bobby had slept through it all, but Brian had been awakened by his mother's cry of surprise when she first caught sight of Trixie. Then just as they were all going to bed, Mr. Lynch had called and had had a long talk with Mr. Belden. So it was nearly dawn by the time the Beldens finished talking and dawn before Trixie fell asleep.

When she and Brian and Mart arrived at the clubhouse they found that Honey and Jim had not heard anything about the exciting events of the night before.

"I thought Di was coming out early to bring you two up to date," Trixie said, propping her eyes open with her fingers. "I myself am too tired and sleepy to talk about it. Di will tell you all about it when she arrives."

"Trixie, *please,*" Honey begged. "How can you expect Jim and me to sit here calmly until Di arrives when all you've told us is that Monty was arrested early this morning? Tell us everything."

Trixie sighed and began at the beginning for what seemed to her about the one hundredth time. "The best part of it all," she finished, "is that Moms and Dad aren't too mad at me."

"They're not mad at all," Brian put in. "They're proud of you, Sis. After all, you didn't *plan* to get yourself kidnaped by Monty."

"I still don't understand about the wire recording machine," Honey complained. "How did it get into the trailer?"

"That's Mart's story," Trixie said wearily. "You have the floor now, Mart."

Mart grinned. "Well, you all know Ty Scott—the guy I was supposed to spend last night with. The recording machine belongs to him. It's his hobby. He belongs to a club and the members send each other records, and all that sort of thing. Like pen pals, you know. Anyway he let me borrow it last night without

242

asking a lot of questions. I put it in my bike basket and carried it out to the Lynches', arriving around nine-fifteen. I knew Monty would be listening to TV in the *Robin* then, so he didn't hear me when I sneaked into the garage and hid on the other side of the limousine. When the program was over, he went into the house and I went into the trailer. I hid the machine under a bunk, plugged it into an outlet, and just as I got everything all set, I happened to glance out of the window and saw Trixie limping barefooted along the driveway. I was so stunned to see her that I just stood there with my mouth open until she turned the handle on the door. It was too late then to shut the machine off. I barely had time to get into the shower compartment and close the door before Trixie walked into the trailer."

Trixie nodded. "That was the click I heard and it scared me to death."

"I don't understand, Mart. Why did you hide from Trixie?" Jim demanded.

"Because," Mart said, "she would have ruined my plan."

"Just what was your plan?" Honey asked. "Whatever could you possibly hope to prove by installing a recorder in the *Robin?*"

"Exactly what I told you at the meeting yesterday afternoon," Mart said. "I planned to get a confession

243

out of Monty, and have it recorded without his knowing anything at all about it."

"I still don't get it," Jim said. "Why should he confess to you in the *Robin* or any place else?"

"Let me tell my story in my own way," Mart pleaded. "I planned to greet him when he came back out to the *Robin* for the eleven o'clock TV show. I was going to confront him with the fact that I had seen him enter Olyfant's hotel both before and after he went to stay with the Lynches. It wasn't true, but it would certainly have shocked him into saying something. I then planned to say that I would not tell on him if he gave me a share of the loot. Ten percent to be exact."

Honey gasped. "Five thousand dollars? Why, Mart, he wouldn't have given you that much money. You didn't have any real proof."

"I didn't expect him to give me any money at all," Mart said patiently. "I simply wanted him to talk, and I think he would have talked plenty under my skillful questioning and cleverly put accusations."

Jim groaned. "And, I suppose, while he was watching you, you would have unplugged the machine, taken it from its hiding place, and walked off with it under your arm? A fat chance you would have had of getting far! You'd have been stopped before you got to the door!"

Mart snapped his fingers. "You forget, my dear James, that I had no idea then that the crook was going to depart that night. I planned to return after he'd gone to bed in the house and remove my equipment then."

"Well, it might have worked at that," Jim admitted. "But you took an awful chance, Mart. He would probably have done the same thing to you that he did to Trixie when he caught her there."

"True," Mart said, "but I didn't know he had a gun. None of us had any idea that he did. If he had tried to get rough with me, lacking a gun, I would have knocked him cold. He's nothing but a flabby-muscled little shrimp, and I guess that's why he does—or did —carry a gun."

"One thing I haven't yet figured out," Trixie said. "Did you plan to leave that machine running until he came back to the *Robin* at eleven? Those spools don't last more than half an hour, do they?"

Mart nodded. "That was luck—sheer luck. I started it in order to test it, and never did turn it off. When the spool runs out, it goes off automatically."

Trixie sighed. "That wasn't the luckiest part of it all. I hate to think about what might have happened to me if you hadn't been hiding in the shower, Mart. Who knows where I'd be now!" She shivered.

Honey gave her an affectionate hug. "It must have been simply awful, Trixie. I would have died of fright."

Jim cleared his throat. "Well, let's call the meeting to order. We can't wait any longer for Di. We must decide today what we're going to do about a clubhouse. Has anybody any ideas?"

At that moment Di burst into the cottage. "Oh, it's all so wonderful," she cried, her pretty face flushed with excitement. "Mother realizes now that none of the strange things that have been happening at our place lately would have happened if she had been running the house the way she used to do. So she's fired Harrison and the nurses, and I'm going to get paid for helping her take care of the twins."

Mart chuckled. "That makes you a fullfledged Bob-White, or should I say fledgling?"

"Speaking of birds," Honey said to Di, "does anyone know what happened to the valuable china ones that disappeared from your father's study?"

Di nodded. "Monty confessed to everything, you know. He stole them and gave them to Olyfant. When the police raided his hotel this morning, they found them in his safe. So this time he *will* go to jail."

"Well," Brian said, "I guess that ties everything up neatly. Except for the Beldens' winter sports equipment." He pointed to the sleds and skis and snowshoes.

247

"There's no room for them in our garage and we can't keep them here any longer. This cottage belongs to Tom and Celia now."

Di laughed. "I forgot to tell you about the reward Dad is giving Trixie and Mart."

"Reward?" Trixie was very wide awake now. "What reward, and why?"

"The *Robin,*" Di said. "Because you kept Monty from getting away with it, not to mention fifty thousand dollars!"

"The *Robin?*" Trixie stared at Mart. "Do you understand what she's talking about?"

"Birds," Mart said. "Bob-Whites and robins and valuable china ones. Not that any of this talk is making much sense to me."

Di giggled. "In words of one syllable, Mart, Dad is giving you and Trixie the red trailer, otherwise known as the *Robin.* And won't it make a wonderful club-house for the Bob-Whites?"

Trixie collapsed in a heap on the dirt floor. "I can't believe it. I just can't believe it. We can't accept it either, can we, Mart?"

"No," he said thoughtfully. "Not for a clubhouse. But we *can* give it to Tom. After all, he played a big part in helping us prove that Monty was an impostor. I, for one, would never have suspected the guy if Tom hadn't told us what he did."

"That's right," Trixie yelled excitedly. "And if you hadn't suspected him I wouldn't he here today. And Monty wouldn't be in jail."

"I guess Tom does deserve a reward, too," Di said. "But do you have to give him the trailer?"

"Heavens, no!" Mart said airily. "We simply make a deal. We keep our clubhouse and he parks the *Robin* on that plot of land Honey was telling us about."

"It's perfect!" Honey clapped her hands. "The ideal spot for the *Robin* is that clearing in the woods on the hill behind the stable. It's got a beautiful view of the Hudson. I'm sure Celia and Tom will be happy about the whole thing, aren't you, Jim?"

"More than happy," Jim agreed. "Boy! Am I ever glad we don't have to give up this place."

Di sighed contentedly. "I've got more news. In that little black notebook which Trixie found in Monty's pocket the police discovered the name and address of my real uncle, my mother's real brother."

"Somehow," Trixie said dreamily, "I always felt sure he was alive."

"He's very much alive," Di said. "Mother telephoned him this morning long distance. He has a huge dude ranch out in Arizona, and he's going to fly east as soon as he can for a happy reunion."

"Why didn't he ever try to get in touch with your mother?" Honey asked.

"He did," Di explained. "But by the time he found out who she was, Dad was rich. Trixie was right about that. My real uncle felt that suddenly showing up then would, well—"

"—make him look like a heel," Mart finished. "Money certainly does complicate things, doesn't it? I'm glad I haven't got any. Except for that dollar Trixie owes me, which amounts to the same thing."

"That's right, rub it in," Trixie said exasperatedly. "Is it my fault I can't pay you back today? Is it my fault I'm not going to get my allowance?"

"Oh, Trixie," Honey cried sympathetically, "why aren't you going to get your allowance?"

"Because," Trixie said ruefully, "Moms and Dad didn't exactly like the idea of my searching Monty's room and the pockets of his coat even if he did turn out to be an impostor."

Brian chuckled. "It's more than that, Sis. The idea is for you to look before you leap into situations which seem perfectly safe, but in your case, almost always turn out to be highly dangerous. In case you've forgotten, you had a narrow escape last night."

Jim sandwiched one of Trixie's hands in both of his and said fondly, "Depriving her of her allowance for one week, I'm afraid, isn't going to change this nitwit. Unless *we* do something drastic about it, I'm afraid she'll end up a pickpocket."

"True, true," Mart said cheerfully. "I think I'll reserve a room for her in Olyfant's hotel right now."

Jim winked at Brian. "She'll never learn unless we punish her. I vote we suspend her from membership in the club for six months."

"Oh, you can't do that," Di cried. "It would ruin everything."

"Why?" Mart demanded. "If we spent less time tracking down crooks, we'd have this clubhouse a showplace before Christmas. Curtains, shelves, cupboards, benches, and tables." He waved his hands. "But instead, because of Trixie, we get a trailer handed to us on a silver platter. Who wants a clubhouse we didn't fix up ourselves? And if we don't suspend Trix we'll never get time to fix this one up."

"Oh, please listen to me," Di begged. "Uncle Monty has invited us all to spend the Christmas holidays at his ranch."

"What?" they all shouted at once. Mart added, "Why didn't you say so before?"

"I've been trying to," Di told him, "but you keep interrupting to tease Trixie. If it's all right with your parents, maybe Dad will charter a plane. Then we could all fly out to Arizona and back, too."

Christmas in Arizona! Brian grabbed Mart's arm excitedly. "Cowboys and Indians and horses galore— why, it'll be like living in a Western movie!"

"And Trixie will probably find us another mystery, even in Arizona," Jim added, smiling at Trixie.

Trixie smiled, too. But deep down inside, she felt that somehow, another exciting mystery was waiting just around the corner. After all, it would be a long time till Christmas!

Trixie